Beyond Time's Veil

OrangeBooks Publication

1st Floor, Rajhans Arcade, Mall Road, Kohka, Bhilai, Chhattisgarh 490020

Website:**www.orangebooks.in**

© Copyright, 2024, Author

All rights reserved. No part of this book may be reproduced, stored in a retrieval system, or transmitted, in any form by any means, electronic, mechanical, magnetic, optical, chemical, manual, photocopying, recording or otherwise, without the prior written consent of its writer.

First Edition, 2024
ISBN: 978-93-6554-097-0

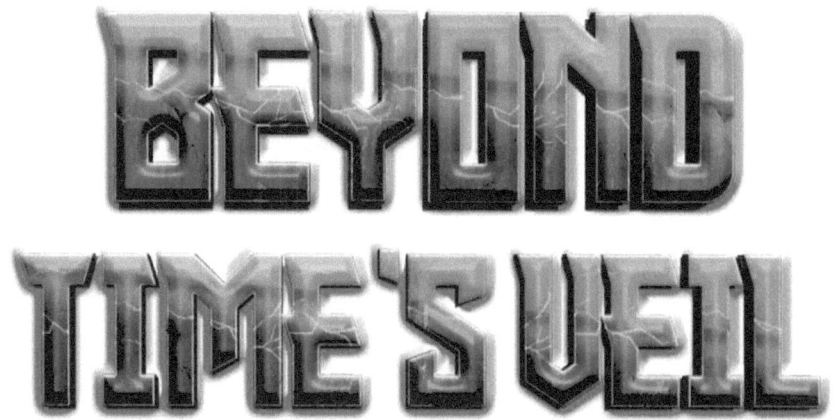

BEYOND TIME'S VEIL

VAISHNAV SHAILESH KAKADE

OrangeBooks Publication
www.orangebooks.in

Dedication

To my beloved Grandfather, whose wisdom and stories were the compass of my dreams. Your guidance and love have been the light that led me through the darkest paths.

Acknowledgements Page

My deepest gratitude goes out to everyone who supported me through this journey. To my family and friends, thank you for your unwavering support and encouragement. To my readers, thank you for joining me on this adventure.

And to my readers, thank you for embarking on this adventure with me.

Preface

As you hold this book in your hands, you're about to dive into a world where time bends, mysteries unfold, and the fabric of reality is woven with both the known and the unknown. But before we begin, I want to take a moment to introduce myself and share the journey that led to the creation of *Beyond Time's Veil*.

I'm **Vaishnav Shailesh Kakade**, and writing has been more than just a passion for me—it's been a lifelong calling. Born and raised in a world filled with curiosity and wonder, I've always been fascinated by the intricacies of science, the complexities of the universe, and the timeless beauty of storytelling. It was the intersection of these fascinations that shaped *Beyond Time's Veil*, a story where imagination meets the boundless possibilities of science and time.

My journey to this point has been deeply influenced by the love and wisdom of my late grandfather, **Shailesh Kakade**. He was a man of immense knowledge, grace, and quiet strength, always encouraging me to seek out the unknown, to challenge the ordinary, and to never shy away from asking the big questions. It's his spirit that runs through the pages of this book, and I can't help but feel that every word written is in part a tribute to him.

But this book isn't just a product of my personal inspirations; it's the culmination of years of learning, experimenting, and understanding the art of storytelling. Throughout the years, I've poured my heart into mastering my craft, always striving to create something unique, something that would resonate with readers on a deeper level. It's my hope that, as you turn these pages, you'll find not just a story of adventure and mystery, but a reflection of your own thoughts, dreams, and desires.

Beyond Time's Veil is the beginning of a larger saga, a journey that will span across realities, challenge the very notion of time, and push the boundaries of what we understand about the universe. The characters you meet here—Alara, Leo, and the mysterious Nexus—are only just beginning their adventure, and I can't wait to take you with them as they discover the secrets that lie beyond the veil.

Writing this book has been an extraordinary experience, and I hope that reading it will be just as rewarding for you. I want this story to do more than entertain—I want it to inspire you, to make you think, to question, and to wonder. There's magic in storytelling, but there's also science, philosophy, and the uncharted territory of our own minds.

I invite you now to step into the world of *Beyond Time's Veil*. Together, we'll explore the mysteries of time and space, the complexities of the human heart, and the ultimate question: what lies beyond the limits of what we know?

Thank you for joining me on this journey. It's one we're going to walk together, and I couldn't be more excited for

what lies ahead.

Vaishnav Shailesh Kakade

Introduction

'Beyond Time's Veil' invites you on a journey through time and space, a testament to the enduring bond between grandparent and grandchild. This novel delves into the essence of heroism, the weight of sacrifice, and the unyielding power of family. May you experience the same wonder and excitement that once illuminated my childhood, guided by my grandfather's tales.

Contents

Chapter - 1
　The Gift 1

Chapter - 2
　The Discovery 20

Chapter - 3
　The Decision 30

Chapter 4
　Chrono Nexus 44

Chapter - 5
　The Timekeepers 63

Chapter - 6
　The First Encounter 69

Chapter - 7
　Allies And Enemies 83

Chapter - 8
　The Hidden Truth 89

Chapter - 9
　The Prophecy 99

Chapter - 10
　The Betrayal 116

Chapter - 11
    The Showdown 121

Chapter - 12
    The Sacrifice 125

Chapter - 13
    The Turning Point 132

Chapter – 14
    Aftermath 136

Chapter - 15
    New Beginnings 140

Chapter – 16
    Reflections 144

Chapter – 17
    The Legacy 150

Chapter - 18
    The Quantum Bond 155

Chapter - 19
    The Veil Between Worlds 217

Chapter - 20
    Epilogue: Echoes of the Unknown 237
Ending Words From The Author 248

Chapter - 1

The Gift

Midnight cloaked the city of New Haven in a blanket of silence, the hum of daily life replaced by the occasional distant siren and the whisper of the wind. Seventeen-year-old Alara Grey stood at her window, feeling like an observer in a world oblivious to the secrets she held. Her ability to see fragments of the future was both a curse and a gift, haunting her dreams and casting a shadow over every waking moment.

The visions came unbidden, fragments of events yet to occur. They were clear as day, unalterable and haunting. These premonitions, though often cryptic, never failed to come true. It was both a gift and a curse, a connection to the fabric of time that her grandmother had once hinted at with her tales of family lore. Her unique ability to glimpse the future set her apart from everyone she knew, but it wasn't always this way. Alara's first vision occurred on a rainy afternoon when she was just ten years old. The scene unfolded in her mind like a movie, predicting an accident at school the next day. When the event came true exactly as she had foreseen, she was left shaken, realizing that her visions were not just dreams, but glimpses into an unchangeable future

Monday greeted New Haven with a dreary, overcast sky, the kind that begged for the warmth of bedcovers and the oblivion of sleep. But Alara had no such luxury; a crucial chemistry exam loomed. She navigated Westbrook High's crowded halls with practiced ease, her mind a whirlwind of chemical equations and the gnawing dread of her next vision.

Hidden in a narrow alley, the old bookstore, Tempus Relics, emerged from the shadows like a forgotten relic. Overgrown ivy draped its entrance, whispering secrets of the past. Alara pushed open the creaky door, releasing a musty aroma that spoke of ancient knowledge and timeworn pages. Inside, towering shelves laden with ancient tomes seemed to reach for the dim, dust-moted light.

For years, Alara kept these visions to herself. At first, they came sporadically—fleeting glimpses of possible futures, always disjointed and unclear. But as she grew older, they became more frequent, more detailed. She began to understand that they were not merely dreams or fantasies but windows into the future, paths she had yet to walk.

It wasn't long before her parents noticed something was different about their daughter. At first, they tried to dismiss her strange behavior as childhood whims, but it became impossible to ignore when Alara accurately predicted events—small accidents, conversations, even the weather. Fear crept into their hearts, though they never voiced it.

Alara felt the weight of their unease. She began to hide her abilities, fearing that the more they knew, the more they would distance themselves from her. In the quiet of her room at night, she would stare into the darkness, wondering why she had been given this gift—or curse.

She could not afford distractions; the nagging sensation that something momentous was imminent gnawed at her focus. Settling into her seat in the classroom, Alara's vision blurred. Suddenly, she found herself in a dark alley, a glowing crystal pulsing coordinated with her heartbeat. The alley was suffocatingly dark, the air thick with tension. A cold gust of wind swept through the narrow passage, carrying with it whispers of the unknown. The glowing crystal in her vision pulsed in sync with her heartbeat, each thrum echoing louder in her mind. Alara's fear and curiosity battled within her, the weight of the unknown pressing on her chest. The overwhelming sense of impending change washed over her. Snapping back to reality, her heart pounded, fully aware that her life was on the brink of transformation. Determined to uncover the truth, Alara resolved to find the crystal. Unbeknownst to her, this quest would thrust her into an adventure that would not only challenge her understanding of time but also her very identity.

Leo noticed her pale face as she approached. "Another vision?" he asked, concern etched deeply into his features. His voice carried the weight of someone who had stood by her side through countless premonitions, each one chipping away at their sense of normalcy.

"Yes, but this one was different. I saw a crystal, and it felt... crucial. We need to find it."

Leo's eyes widened. "A crystal? Do you think it is connected to your abilities?"

"I do not know why, but I have a feeling it is essential. We need to start looking now."

Determined to uncover the truth, Alara and Leo set off after school. They navigated the bustling streets of New Haven, heading towards the city's oldest district. Known for its historic buildings and hidden secrets, this area tugged at Alara's intuition, urging her forward with a certainty she could not ignore.

Tucked away in a narrow alley, the old bookstore, Tempus Relics, emerged from the shadows like a forgotten relic. Overgrown ivy draped its entrance, whispering secrets of the past. Alara pushed open the creaky door, releasing a musty aroma of ancient books and hidden knowledge. Alara pushed open the creaky door, and they stepped inside. The musty aroma of old books filled the air, and shelves lined with ancient tomes towered over them. The sign above the door read "Tempus Relics." Inside, the shop was a maze of curiosities from different eras, each item whispering tales of the past. "Look at this place," Leo marvelled, his eyes scanning the relics. "If there's any place to find a mysterious crystal, it's here."

They entered, and the bell above the door chimed softly. An elderly man behind the counter looked up, his eyes sharp and knowing. "Good afternoon. Can I help you with something?"

Alara hesitated, then decided to be honest. "I am looking for a crystal. It is small, and it glows. I know it sounds strange, but..."

The elderly man's eyes sparkled with a mix of curiosity and wisdom. "You seek the Chrono Crystal," he said, his voice a soft whisper that carried an unspoken warning. "Many have come searching for it, but few understand its true power." He paused, scrutinizing Alara and Leo as if measuring their worthiness. "The crystal chooses its own bearer, and the path to it is fraught with peril."

He disappeared into the back room, leaving Alara and Leo to look around. The shop was filled with artifacts, each one more fascinating than the last. The dim lighting cast eerie shadows across the room, and the sound of a distant clock ticking added to the sense of timelessness. Dust motes danced in the slivers of light that pierced through the cracked windows. Each step Alara took seemed to echo with the weight of history.

After a few tense minutes, the shopkeeper returned, cradling a small wooden box with an air of reverence. He placed it gently on the counter and opened it, revealing a mesmerizing, glowing crystal. It pulsed with an ethereal light, exactly as Alara had envisioned.

"This is the Chrono Crystal," the shopkeeper explained. "It is said to possess the power to manipulate time. It has been in my family for generations, but it is not for sale. Why do you seek it?"

Alara reached out to touch the crystal, and the moment her fingers made contact, she felt a surge of energy course through her body. Images flashed before her eyes – past, present, and future intertwining in a chaotic dance. She pulled her hand back, breathing heavily.

"I need it," she said firmly. "I do not know why, but it is important. It is connected to my abilities."

The shopkeeper studied her for a moment, then nodded. "Very well. If you honestly believe you are meant to have it, I will entrust it to you. But be warned – the power of the Chrono Crystal is not to be taken lightly. It comes with great responsibility."

Alara accepted the crystal with a blend of awe and trepidation. The uncertainty of what lay ahead loomed large, yet she knew this was merely the dawn of her journey. As they delved deeper into the bookstore, a sense of unease settled over them. Alara glanced at Leo, who seemed equally on edge. The elderly man's words echoed in her mind, and she could not shake the feeling that they were being watched. Suddenly, a loud crash shattered the silence, and they spun around to see a shadowy figure darting through the aisles. "We're not alone," Alara whispered, her heart pounding. "We need to find that crystal before they do."

As they left the shop, Leo looked at her with a mixture of excitement and concern.

"What now?" he asked.

"Now," Alara said, her voice steady and resolute, "we uncover what this crystal can do. And prepare for whatever comes next."

On her sixteenth birthday, the visions intensified. No longer did she see only fragments; now, entire moments of the future played out before her eyes. Each time she closed her eyes, a different scene unfolded—some beautiful, others terrifying. But one thing remained constant: the crystal.

It appeared in every vision, always resting in her hand, always glowing with an ethereal light. Alara began to feel its weight even when it wasn't there, as though it were calling to her, waiting for her to claim it. The old man from her first vision returned as well, his warnings growing more urgent.

"You must keep it safe, Alara. The future depends on it."

Despite the increasing frequency of her visions, Alara had learned to live with them—until the day the vision changed. It was no longer just the future she saw, but the past as well. She saw her ancestors, generations of people she had never met but whose lives were somehow intertwined with hers. They, too, had carried the crystal, protecting it, safeguarding its power.

But with the past came knowledge of a dark force—an ancient enemy who had pursued the crystal through the ages, seeking its power for himself. His name was Veridian, and he would stop at nothing to claim it.

The vision left her trembling. For the first time in years, Alara felt truly afraid. This was not just about her anymore; it was about something much larger, something that spanned centuries. The weight of responsibility settled on her shoulders like a heavy cloak.

The next few days were a whirlwind of research and revelations. Leo used his tech skills to scour online databases, while Alara poured overold books and documents, piecing together the history of the Chrono Crystal. Their search led them to a reclusive historian named Professor Thorne, rumoured to know more about ancient relics than anyone else in New Haven.

Professor Thorne lived in a secluded mansion on the outskirts of the city, a place shrouded in mystery and tales of the supernatural. As they approached the imposing gates, Leo voiced his doubts. "Are you sure about this?"

"We don't have a choice," Alara replied. "If anyone can help us understand the crystal, it's him."

They rang the bell, and moments later, a tall, gaunt man with piercing eyes answered the door. "Yes? What is it?" he asked brusquely.

"Professor Thorne, my name is Alara Grey, and this is my friend Leo. We need your help with something important," Alara said, holding up the Chrono Crystal.

The professor's eyes widened with recognition. "The Chrono Crystal... Come in, quickly."

They followed him into a cluttered study filled with books, artifacts, and strange devices. Thorne gestured for them to sit, then examined the crystal closely.

"Where did you find this?" he asked, his voice a mix of awe and curiosity.

"An antique shop in the old district," Alara replied. "I saw it in a vision. It is connected to my ability to see the future."

Thorne nodded slowly. "The Chrono Crystal is a powerful artifact, said to be created by an ancient civilization with advanced knowledge of time manipulation. It can bend time, allowing the user to see and even alter the past and future. But such power comes with significant risk."

"What kind of risk?" Leo asked, leaning forward.

"The crystal can be unstable, especially if used improperly. It can create time paradoxes, altering events in unpredictable

ways. And there are those who would seek to control its power for their own purposes," Thorne explained.

Alara felt a chill run down her spine. "Like whom?"

"The Timekeepers," Thorne said, his expression darkening. "A secret organization that has existed for centuries. They seek to control the flow of time and rewrite history to their advantage. If they get their direct the Chrono Crystal, the consequences could be catastrophic."

Alara and Leo exchanged worried glances. "What do we do?" Alara asked.

Thorne looked at her with a serious expression. "You must learn to control the crystal and protect it from falling into the wrong hands. There are others like you, with abilities connected to time. You need to find them and join forces."

"Where do we start?" Leo asked.

"There are rumours of a hidden realm called the Chrono Nexus, where time is fluid and the past, present, and future intertwine. If the legends are true, it could hold the key to unlocking the full potential of the Chrono Crystal and defeating the Timekeepers," Thorne said.

Alara took a deep breath, feeling the weight of their mission. "Then we need to find the Chrono Nexus."

Thorne nodded. "I will help you as much as I can but be careful. The journey will be dangerous, and the stakes are higher than you can imagine."

As they left Thorne Manor, Alara felt a renewed sense of purpose. She knew the road ahead would be fraught with challenges, but she was determined to protect the crystal and prevent the Timekeepers from rewriting history.

That night, Alara could not sleep. The Chrono Crystal sat on her bedside table, glowing softly in the darkness. She reached out to touch it, and as soon as her fingers brushed its surface, a vision overtook her. She saw a vast, otherworldly landscape, filled with swirling energy and ancient ruins. In the distance, a grand, shimmering portal beckoned – the entrance to the Chrono Nexus.

The vision was more vivid than any she had experienced before. She felt the cool air of the Nexus on her skin, heard the distant echoes of ancient voices, and sensed the immense power that lay within.

As the vision faded, Alara found herself back in her dimly lit bedroom, her heart racing. She knew that whatever awaited her in the Chrono Nexus was crucial, not just for her but for the fabric of time itself. The weight of responsibility pressed down on her shoulders, but she steeled herself, determined to face whatever challenges lay ahead.

From that day forward, Alara knew she could not ignore the visions any longer. The crystal was real, and it was calling to her. She had to find it before Veridian did.

Armed with little more than the knowledge of her visions and the faintest idea of where to start, Alara set out on her journey. She left behind the safety of her home, stepping into the unknown with nothing but a vague sense of purpose to guide her.

But even as she walked away from the life she had known, she couldn't shake the feeling that she was being watched. The air around her felt charged, as though time itself was bending and shifting in ways she didn't understand. Every step she took brought her closer to the crystal—and to the dangers that awaited her.

The next morning, Alara and Leo met early at their favourite coffee shop, a cozy nook tucked away from the main street. The aroma of freshly brewed coffee mingled with the scent of pastries, providing a comforting backdrop to their urgent conversation.

"We need to prepare," Alara said, her voice steady. "The vision I had lastnight was intense. I saw the entrance to the Chrono Nexus, and I felt its power. We have to find it and figure out how to use it."

Leo nodded; his expression serious. "We need more information. Thorne mentioned others like you with abilities connected to time. We should tryto find them. Maybe they can help us."

Alara agreed, and they decided to divide their efforts. Leo would continue his digital search for any clues about the Chrono Nexus and others with time-related abilities, while Alara would visit the old libraries and archives in the city, hoping to uncover more about the crystal and its history.

After school, Alara could not shake the image of the crystal from her mind. Drawn to the library, she began searching through the dusty old tomes for any mention of such a crystal. Hours passed, and just as she was about to give up, a passage caught her eye: "The Chrono Crystal, an artifact of immense power, is said to control the very fabric of time. Its whereabouts are unknown, and many have perished in its pursuit." Alara's heart raced as she realized the gravity of her discovery. The librarian, an elderly woman with kind eyes and a wealth of information, greeted them warmly.

"How can I assist you today?" she asked.

"We're looking for any records or books about a place called the Chrono Nexus," Alara explained. "And anything about a crystal known as the Chrono Crystal."

The librarian's eyes widened slightly at the mention of the Chrono Crystal. "Follow me," she said, leading them to a secluded section of the library where dusty volumes lined the shelves. "This section contains texts on ancient relics and mystical places. You might find what you're looking for here."

Alara and Leo spent hours poring over old manuscripts and scrolls. They discovered tales of the Chrono Nexus, described as a realm where time was fluid and interconnected. According to the texts, the Nexus was guarded by powerful beings known as the Chronomancies, who possessed the ability to manipulate time.

As they delved deeper, they found references to a prophecy about a chosen one who would wield the Chrono Crystal to protect the timeline from those who sought to alter it. The chosen one was said to have visions of the future, guiding them to their destiny.

"Alara, this sounds like you," Leo said, excitement in his voice. "You have the visions. Maybe you are the chosen one."

Alara felt a mixture of fear and determination. "If that's true, then we have to find the Chrono Nexus and the Chronomancies. They can teach me how to control the crystal."

Their research also uncovered mentions of a secret society known as the Timekeepers, dedicated to controlling the flow of time for their own purposes. The texts warned that the Timekeepers were relentless in their pursuit of the Chrono Crystal and would stop at nothing to seize its power.

"We need to be careful," Alara said, her voice low. "The Timekeepers aredangerous. We can't let them get the crystal."

As they left the library, Alara's mind raced with the added information. The weight of her responsibility felt heavier, but she was more determined than ever to protect the crystal and uncover the secrets of the Chrono Nexus.

The next few days were a blur of research and planning. Alara and Leo worked tirelessly, driven by the urgency of their mission. They uncovered more clues about the Chrono Nexus, learning that the entrancewas hidden in a place where time seemed to stand still.

One evening, as they were reviewing their findings, a mysterious message appeared on Leo's computer screen. It was an invitation to a secret meeting of individuals with unique abilities, much like Alara's.The message promised answers and guidance.

"This could be our chance," Leo said, his eyes gleaming with excitement."We need to go to this meeting. It might be dangerous, but it's our best lead."

Alara agreed, though a sense of unease settled in her stomach. The meeting was scheduled for the following night, in an abandoned warehouse on the outskirts of the city.

The next evening, they approached the warehouse cautiously. The building loomed ominously in the darkness, its windows shattered, and its walls covered in graffiti. They slipped inside, their footsteps echoing in the vast, empty space.

Inside, they found a small group of people gathered around a flickering lantern. Each person radiated a unique aura, hinting at their extraordinary abilities. A tall, enigmatic figure stepped forward, his eyes glinting with curiosity.

"Welcome," he said, his voice smooth and commanding. "I am Eamon, the leader of this group. We have been waiting for you, Alara Grey."

Alara's heart skipped a beat. "How do you know who I am?"

Eamon smiled. "We have our ways. We know about your visions and the Chrono Crystal. You are not alone in this fight."

The group introduced themselves, each revealing their own unique abilities. There was Mara, who could manipulate shadows, and Jaxon, who could bend metal with his mind. They had a common purpose together drawn all: to protect the timeline from those who would seek to corrupt it.

Eamon explained that they had been watching the Timekeepers for years, thwarting their attempts to alter momentous events in history. They had been waiting for someone with Alara's abilities, someone who could wield the Chrono Crystal and tip the balance in their favour.

"You have a great power, Alara," Eamon said. "But you also have a great responsibility. The Timekeepers are growing stronger, and the fabric of time is at risk. We must find the Chrono Nexus and harness its power to stop them."

Alara felt a surge of determination. "I want to help. I need to learn how to control the crystal and fulfil my destiny."

Eamon nodded. "Then we will train you. But first, we need to find the entrance to the Chrono Nexus. It is hidden in a place where time stands still, a place that defies the laws of physics."

Leo's eyes lit up. "I think I know where that might be. There is an old clock tower on the edge of town. It has been stuck at the same time for decades. Maybe that's the place."

Eamon smiled. "It's worth investigating. We leave at dawn."

As the group dispersed to prepare for the journey, Alara felt a sense of belonging she had never experienced before. She was no longer alone in her quest. She had allies, people who understood her abilities and shared her mission.

At dawn, the group gathered at the old clock tower. The building was a relic of the past, its hands frozen in time. As they approached, Alara felt a familiar pull, the same energy she had felt in her visions.

"This is it," she said, her voice trembling with excitement. "The entrance to the Chrono Nexus."

Eamon stepped forward, his eyes scanning the tower. "The entrance is hidden. We need to find a way to reveal it."

Mara moved closer, her hands weaving shadows into intricate patterns. "I can sense a hidden mechanism. It is protected by an ancient spell. Alara, you need to use the crystal."

Alara took a deep breath and held the Chrono Crystal in her hand. Its glow intensified, illuminating the hidden symbols carved into the tower's stone walls. She closed her eyes and focused, letting the energy of the crystal guide her.

Suddenly, the ground beneath them rumbled, and a hidden door slowly creaked open, revealing a dark, winding staircase. Alara felt a surge of triumph mixed with trepidation.

"This is it," she said, her voice steady. "The entrance to the Chrono Nexus."

The group descended the staircase, their hearts pounding with anticipation. As they reached the bottom, they found themselves in a vast, otherworldly chamber filled with swirling energy and ancient ruins.

In the centre of the chamber stood the grand, shimmering portal Alara had seen in her vision. The air crackled with power, and the distant echoes of ancient voices filled the space.

Eamon turned to Alara; his eyes filled with determination. "This is your destiny, Alara. You must enter the Chrono Nexus and unlock its secrets. The fate of the timeline depends on you."

Alara took a deep breath, her heart filled with resolve. She stepped forward, ready to embrace her destiny and the immense power that lay within the Chrono Nexus.

Chapter - 2
The Discovery

As dawn broke, Alara and her newfound allies gathered at the base of the ancient clock tower. Morning fog clung to the ground, shrouding their meeting in an air of mystery. Clutching the glowing Chrono Crystal, Alara felt a surge of destiny, a mixture of thrill and terror coursing through her veins.

Eamon, their enigmatic leader, stepped forward, his commanding presence capturing everyone's attention. "This is it," he said, his voice low but powerful. "The entrance to the Chrono Nexus lies within. Remember, once we enter, there is no turning back."

Alara glanced at Leo, who gave her a reassuring nod. She took a deep breath and stepped towards the hidden door that had revealed itself in the clock tower's stone wall. With a gentle push, the door creaked open, revealing a dark, winding staircase.

"Stay close and be prepared for anything," Eamon instructed as they began their descent.

The stairs seemed to go on forever, spiralling deeper into the earth. The air grew cooler, and the walls were lined with ancient symbols that glowed faintly in the darkness. Alara could not shake the feeling that they were being watched, but she pressed on, determined to uncover the secrets of the Chrono Nexus.

After what felt like an eternity, they reached the bottom of the staircase. A massive cavern stretched out before them, filled with swirling energy and ancient ruins. In the centre of the cavern stood the grand, shimmering portal Alara had seen in her vision.

"This is it," Alara whispered, her voice filled with awe.

Eamon nodded. "The Chrono Nexus. It is more magnificent than I imagined."

Suddenly, a figure emerged from the shadows. It was a "Welcome, Alara Grey," the woman said, her voice echoing through the cavern. "I am Seraphina, a guardian of the Chrono Nexus. We have been expecting you."

Alara's heart pounded in her chest. "How do you know who I am?"

Seraphina smiled. "The Nexus reveals many things. You are the chosen one, destined to protect the timeline. But you are not alone in this fight. We are here to guide you."

Eamon stepped forward, his eyes narrowing. "And what of the Timekeepers? They seek to control the crystal and alter history for their own gain."

Seraphina's expression grew serious. "The Timekeepers are a formidable foe, but they can be defeated. To do so, you must unlock the full potential of the Chrono Crystal and learn to harness its power."

Alara felt a surge of determination. "How do we do that?"

Seraphina gestured to the portal. "Enter the Nexus, and your journey will begin. You will face many trials, but they are necessary to unlock your true potential."

Without hesitation, Alara stepped towards the portal, the crystal glowing brightly in her hand. As she crossed the threshold, a wave of energy enveloped her, and she felt herself being pulled into another realm.

Alara found herself standing in a vast, ethereal landscape. The sky was a swirling mass of colours, and the ground beneath her feet glowed with an otherworldly light. She could see the faint outlines of ancient structures and statues, their features worn by time.

Leo appeared beside her, looking equally awestruck. "This place is incredible."

Eamon and the rest of the group followed, each one taking in the sights with a mixture of wonder and trepidation. Seraphina appeared before them; her presence more tangible in this realm.

"Welcome to the Chrono Nexus," she said. "Here, time is fluid, and the past, present, and future are intertwined. To unlock the power of the crystal, you must first understand the nature of time itself."

She led them to a large, circular platform in the centre of the Nexus. "This is the Platform of Reflections," Seraphina explained. "It will reveal to you the key moments in your life and the choices that have shaped your destiny. Only by confronting these moments can you gain the strength to face the trials ahead."

One by one, they stepped onto the platform. As Alara stood in the centre, the platform began to glow, and images from her past flickered around her. She saw herself as a child, discovering her ability to see the future for the first time. She saw her grandmother, who had hinted at their family's connection to the fabric of time. She saw the day she met Leo and the bond they had formed.

Each image brought a flood of emotions, but Alara faced them with determination. She knew that understanding her past was crucial to mastering the power of the crystal.

When the images faded, Seraphina spoke again. "You have confronted your past, but now you must face the future. The Timekeepers will stop at nothing to seize the crystal. You must be ready."

Suddenly, the ground beneath them trembled, and a portal opened on the far side of the platform. Dark figures emerged, their cloaks billowing like shadows.

"The Timekeepers," Eamon said, drawing his weapon. "Prepare yourselves."

A fierce battle ensued, with Alara and her allies fighting valiantly against the Timekeepers. The air crackled with energy as spells and weapons clashed. Alara held the crystal tightly, using its power to fend off their attackers.

During the chaos, Alara felt a surge of strength and clarity. She realized that the crystal was not just a tool, but an extension of herself. With this newfound understanding, she unleashed a powerful wave of energy that sent the Timekeepers reeling.

The battle ended as quickly as it had begun, the Timekeepers retreating into the shadows. Alara's heart pounded in her chest, but she felt a sense of triumph.

"You have done well," Seraphina said, her voice filled with pride. "But this is only the beginning. The true test lies ahead."

Alara nodded, determination burning in her eyes. "I am ready. Whatever it takes to protect the timeline, I will do it."

As they ventured deeper into the Nexus, they encountered more trials designed to assess their resolve and abilities. They faced illusions that challenged their perception of reality, puzzles that required them to think freely, and battles that pushed them to their limits.

Through it all, Alara felt herself growing stronger. She learned to harness the power of the crystal with greater precision and control, using it to manipulate time in ways she had never thought possible. She also grew closer to her allies, their bond strengthening with each challenge they overcame.

One night, as they rested by a shimmering lake, Alara and Leo sat together, reflecting on their journey.

"Do you ever wonder what our lives would be like if we didn't havethese abilities?" Leo asked, his voice thoughtful.

Alara nodded. "Sometimes. But then I remember why we are doing this. We have a responsibility to protect the timeline and ensure that history unfolds as it should."

Leo smiled. "You are right. And I am glad we're in this together."

As they gazed at the stars, Alara felt a sense of peace. Despite the challenges they faced, she knew they were on the right path.

The next morning, Seraphina led them to a towering structure in the heart of the Nexus. "This is the Tower of Time," she said. "At its peak lies the Chamber of Eternity, where the true power of the crystal can be unlocked. But beware, the Timekeepers heavily guard the tower."

As they ascended the tower, they encountered fierce resistance. The Timekeepers were relentless, using every trick and tactic at their disposal to stop them. But Alara and her allies fought with determination, their skills honed by the trials they had faced.

When they finally reached the top, they found themselves in a grand chamber filled with swirling energy. At the centre of the chamber stood a pedestal, upon which the Chrono Crystal pulsed with a radiant light.

Seraphina stepped forward. "This is it, Alara. The decisive moment. Place the crystal on the pedestal and unlock its full potential."

With trembling hands, Alara approached the pedestal and placed the crystal upon it. The chamber was bathed in a brilliant light, and Alara felt a surge of power unlike anything she had ever experienced.

Visions of the past, present, and future flooded her mind, and she saw the intricate web of time stretching out before her. She understood now that her role was not just to protect the timeline, but to guide it, ensuring that history unfolded as it was meant to.

As the light faded, Alara felt a sense of clarity and purpose. She turned to her allies, her eyes shining with determination. "We did it. We unlocked the power of the crystal. Now, we must use it to stop the Timekeepers and protect the timeline."

Eamon nodded; his expression filled with pride. "You have become a true guardian of time, Alara. The future is in your hands."

With renewed resolve, Alara and her allies prepared to face their greatest challenge yet: a final showdown with the Timekeepers. They knew the battle ahead would be fierce, but they were ready to fight for the future and ensure that history remained intact.

As they left the Tower of Time, Alara could not help but feel a sense of hope. The journey had been long and arduous, but they had grown stronger with each step. They were not just a group of individuals with unique abilities; they were a family, united by a common purpose.

The Chrono Nexus had revealed its secrets, and Alara knew that they were ready to face whatever challenges lay ahead.

With the power of the crystal and the strength of their bonds, they would confront the Timekeepers and secure the future of the timeline.

As they descended from the Tower of Time, Seraphina led them to a hidden alcove within the Nexus. Inside, they found a vast repository of ancient scrolls and artifacts, each one detailing the history and secrets of time itself.

"These scrolls contain the knowledge of the Chronomancies," Seraphina explained. "Study them well, for they will aid you in the battles to come."

Alara and her friends spent days pouring over the scrolls, absorbing the wisdom of the ancient guardians. They learned about the origins of the Chrono Crystal, its connection to the fabric of time, and the intricate workings of the Nexus. Each piece of knowledge they uncovered brought them closer to understanding their mission and the true nature of their powers.

During their studies, they discovered references to an ancient artifact known as the Temporal Key, a powerful relic capable of sealing the Chrono Crystal and preventing it from falling into the wrong hands. The scrolls hinted that the key was hidden somewhere within the Nexus, guarded by the most formidable of the Timekeepers.

"This key could be our only chance to secure the crystal and end the Timekeepers' threat once and for all," Alara said, her determination renewed. "We need to find it."

Their search for the Temporal Key led them to a remote part of the Nexus, a place where the boundaries of time and space seemed to blur. The landscape was surreal, with floating islands, shifting pathways, and shimmering portals that led to different points in history.

As they navigated the treacherous terrain, they encountered numerous challenges, from temporal distortions that threatened to trap them in different eras to spectral guardians that assessed their resolve. Through it all, they relied on their newfound knowledge and the strength of their bond to guide them.

One night, as they made camp on a floating island, Alara had a vision. She saw the location of the Temporal Key, hidden within a temple at the heart of a time vortex. The vision was vivid and clear, and she knew it was their next destination.

"The key is within our reach," Alara announced to the group. "We just need to make it through the vortex."

The journey to the temple was fraught with danger. The time vortex was a chaotic swirl of energy, pulling them in different directions and distorting their perception of reality. But Alara, with the crystal's guidance, led them through, her determination unwavering.

When they finally reached the temple, they found it guarded by a formidable Timekeeper, a tall, imposing figure with eyes that seemed to pierce through time itself. The Timekeeper wielded a staff that crackled with temporal energy, ready to defend the key at all costs.

"This is it," Eamon said, drawing his weapon. "We must defeat the guardian and secure the key."

A fierce battle ensued, with the Timekeeper unleashing waves of temporal energy that distorted time and space around them. Alara and her allies fought bravely, using everything they had learned to counter the Timekeeper's attacks. The air crackled with energy as spells and weapons clashed, each strike resonating with the power of the Nexus.

During the battle, Alara felt the crystal pulsing with a familiar energy. She realized that the key to defeating the Timekeeper lay in her connection to the crystal and the timeline. Focusing all her strength, she channelled the crystal's power, creating a shield that deflected the Timekeeper's attacks and turned the tide of the battle.

With a final surge of energy, Alara struck the Timekeeper with a blast of temporal force, disarming him and sending him reeling. The guardian fell to the ground, defeated, and the temple fell silent.

Chapter - 3
The Decision

The promise of adventure loomed large as Alara, and her allies stood at the base of the Tower of Time. Each challenge they had faced had forged them stronger, yet their journey was far from over. With the Chrono Crystal's power unlocked, the immense responsibility of protecting the timeline from the Timekeepers now rested heavily upon them.

Alara turned to her friends, her eyes filled with determination. "We have unlocked the power of the crystal, but our mission isn't complete. We must find the Temporal Key and secure the timeline finally."

Leo nodded; his expression serious. "We are with you, Alara. Whateverit takes."

Eamon stepped forward, his presence commanding as always. "Our next step is to locate the key. The Nexus has revealed its secrets to us, but we must use that knowledge wisely."

Seraphina, the guardian of the Chrono Nexus, approached them. "The Temporal Key is hidden within a temple at the heart of a time vortex. The journey will be perilous, but you have the strength and the power to succeed."

Alara felt a surge of determination. "Then let's go. The future dependson us."

As they prepared for the journey, Alara couldn't help but reflect on the trials they had faced. Each challenge had brought them closer together, forging bonds that could not be broken. The power of the crystal had given them the strength to overcome any obstacle, and she knew that they were ready for whatever lay ahead.

The journey to the time vortex was a harrowing ordeal, the landscape shifting and changing like a living entity. Each step brought new dangers: temporal distortions threatening to ensnare them in different eras. Alara's mastery over the crystal became their beacon, guiding them safely through the chaotic terrain.

As they approached the vortex, the very air seemed to hum with energy. The sky above them twisted and swirled, a chaotic mix of colours and light. It was a breathtaking sight, but also a reminder of the power they were about to confront.

"We're close," Seraphina said, her voice steady. "The temple lies at the heart of the vortex. Be prepared for anything."

Alara took a deep breath, her resolve unwavering. "We're ready."

The entrance to the vortex was like stepping into another dimension. The ground beneath their feet seemed to shift and bend, and the pull of gravity was unlike anything they had ever experienced. It was as if they were walking on the edge of a black hole, where the laws of physics were constantly in flux.

Leo, ever the science enthusiast, couldn't help but marvel at their surroundings. "This is incredible. It's like we're inside a singularity, where time and space are intertwined. Einstein's theories of general relativity are at play here."

Eamon nodded. "Stay focused. The vortex is unstable, and we need to reach the temple before it collapses."

With the Chrono Crystal guiding their way, they navigated the treacherous landscape. The path was filled with floating islands, shifting pathways, and temporal anomalies that threatened to pull them into different eras. But Alara's control over the crystal kept them on course.

After what felt like an eternity, they finally reached the temple. It was an ancient structure, its walls covered in glowing symbols and intricate carvings. The energy within the temple was palpable, a testament to the power it held.

"This is it," Seraphina said. "The Temporal Key is inside. Be cautious, for it is heavily guarded."

As they entered the temple, they encountered a formidable Timekeeper Guardian. The guardian was a tall, imposing figure with eyes that seemed to pierce through time itself. He wielded a staff that crackled with temporal energy, ready to defend the key at all costs.

A fierce battle ensued, with the guardian unleashing waves of temporal energy that distorted time and space around them. Alara and her allies fought bravely, using everything they had learned to counter the guardian's attacks. The air crackled with energy as spells and weapons clashed.

Amid the chaos, Alara felt the crystal pulsing with a familiar energy. She realized that the key to defeating the guardian lay in her connection to the crystal and the timeline. Focusing all her strength, she channelled the crystal's power, creating a shield that deflected the guardian's attacks and turned the tide of the battle.

With a final surge of energy, Alara struck the guardian with a blast of temporal force, disarming him and sending him reeling. The guardian fell to the ground, defeated, and the temple fell silent.

Alara approached the pedestal in the centre of the temple, where the Temporal Key rested. She reached out and grasped the key, feeling a surge of power as it resonated with the crystal.

"We did it," she said, her voice filled with relief. "We have the key."

Seraphina stepped forward; her eyes filled with pride. "You have proven yourselves worthy. The Temporal Key will allow you to secure the crystal and protect the timeline from the Timekeepers."

Alara nodded, her eyes blazing with determination. "We will stop them, once and for all," she vowed, her voice steady and unwavering.

The final showdown with the Timekeepers unfolded at the heart of the Chrono Nexus, where the threads of time converged, and the fate of the timeline hung in the balance. Alara and her allies stood poised, their resolve unbreakable.

The Timekeepers emerged from the shadows, their leader, a figure cloaked in darkness, stepping forward. "You cannot stop us," the leader said, his voice echoing through the Nexus. "We will control the timeline and reshape history as we see fit."

Alara stepped forward, the Chrono Crystal and the Temporal Key in hand. "You are wrong. We will protect the timeline and ensure that history unfolds as it should."

The battle that followed was fierce and relentless. The air crackled with energy as spells and weapons clashed, each side fighting with everything they had. Alara and her allies used the knowledge they had gained and the power of the crystal to counter the Timekeepers' attacks, their determination fuelling their strength.

Amid the chaos, Alara felt a surge of power from the crystal. She realized that the key to defeating the Timekeepers lay in their connection to the timeline and their understanding of its true nature.

With the Temporal Key in hand, she channelled the crystal's power, creating a barrier that deflected the Timekeepers' attacks and began to unravel their control over time. The leader of the Timekeepers, realizing his defeat, made one last desperate attempt to seize the crystal, but Alara was ready.

Using the combined power of the crystal and the key, she unleashed a wave of temporal energy that engulfed the leader, disintegrating his form and breaking the Timekeepers' hold on the timeline.

As the energy faded, the Nexus fell silent. The Timekeepers had been defeated, and the timeline was secure.

Alara turned to her allies, her expression filled with relief and pride. "We did it. The timeline is safe."

Seraphina stepped forward; her eyes filled with gratitude.

"You have proven yourselves true guardians of time. The future is in your hands."

With the Chrono Crystal and the Temporal Key secured, Alara and her allies returned to the Nexus, their mission complete. They had faced incredible challenges and emerged stronger; their bond unbreakable.

As they stood together, gazing at the swirling energy of the Nexus, Alara felt a sense of peace. The journey had been long and arduous, but they had succeeded. They had protected the timeline and ensured that history would unfold as it was meant to.

And as they looked to the future, they knew that whatever challenges lay ahead, they would face them together, as guardians of time.

As guardians of time, Alara and her allies knew their responsibilities extended far beyond the Chrono Nexus. The timeline was a fragile entity, and any disturbance could have catastrophic effects. They needed to be vigilant and proactive, ensuring that history unfolded as it should.

Seraphina, the wise guardian, addressed the group with a sense of urgency. "Now that you possess the Temporal Key and the Chrono Crystal, you must understand the complexities of time travel and the fundamental laws of the universe. The next part of your journey will test your knowledge and your ability to apply it."

Alara felt a mix of excitement and apprehension. "What do we need to know?"

Seraphina gestured to a nearby portal. *"The Nexus will take you to different realms where the laws of physics are paramount. You will encounter phenomena that challenge your understanding of time, space, and light. Your first destination is the Realm of Optics, wherethe manipulation of light is key to your success."*

With a deep breath, Alara led the group through the portal. They emerged in a dazzling world where light bent and twisted in ways that defied logic. Rainbows arched across the sky, and beams of light danced around them, creating patterns that seemed to shift with every step.

Leo's eyes sparkled with wonder. "This is incredible. It's like we're insidea giant prism."

Eamon nodded; his expression serious. "Remember, we need to understand how light works here to move forward."

Seraphina's voice echoed in their minds. "In the Realm of Optics, you must use the principles of light reflection and refraction to navigate the terrain. Mirrors and lenses will be your tools."

Alara looked around, spotting a series of mirrors and lenses scattered throughout the landscape. She picked up convex lens and held it up to the light, watching as the beams converged to a single point.

"We can use these to direct the light," she said, a plan forming in her mind. "If we position the mirrors and lenses correctly, we can create a path to the next portal."

Leo and Eamon quickly got to work, adjusting the mirrors and lenses under Alara's guidance. They used the principles of reflection, where light bounces off a surface at the same angle it arrives, and refraction, where light bends when it passes through a different medium.

As they worked, Leo explained the concepts in simple terms. "When light hits a mirror, it reflects at the same angle it came in. And when it goes through a lens, it bends. A convex lens makes the light converge, while a concave lens makes it diverge."

Eamon nodded. "It's like solving a puzzle with light."

With the mirrors and lenses in place, they created a path of light beams that led to the next portal. The beams danced and twisted, illuminating their way forward. Alara stepped onto the path, the Chrono Crystal glowing brightly in her hand.

"Let's go," she said, her voice filled with determination.

They followed the path of light, navigating through the dazzling landscape. The principles of optics guided them,

and they felt a sense of accomplishment as they reached the next portal.

"Well done," Seraphina's voice echoed. "You have mastered the Realm of Optics. Your next destination is the Realm of Relativity, where the flow of time is as fluid as water."

They stepped through the portal and emerged in a world where the very fabric of time seemed to bend and twist. The sky was a swirling vortex of colours, and the ground beneath their feet seemed to shift with every step.

Leo looked around in awe. "This place... it's like we're in the middle of a time warp."

Seraphina's voice guided them. "In the Realm of Relativity, you must understand the principles of time dilation and the effects of gravity on time. Time moves differently here, and you must navigate this realm by understanding how time and space are intertwined."

Alara felt a surge of determination. "We need to find the key to navigating this realm."

As they moved forward, they encountered pockets of slow and fast time, where the flow of time varied dramatically. In some areas, seconds stretched into minutes, while in others, minutes passed in the blink of an eye.

Leo explained the concept of time dilation. "According to Einstein's theory of relativity, time moves slower in stronger gravitational fields. It's like how time moves slower near a black hole compared to Earth."

Eamon nodded. "So, we need to find the areas where time flows normally to move forward."

They used their understanding of time dilation to navigate the realm, moving carefully through areas where time flowed at different rates. Alara used the Chrono Crystal to sense the flow of time, guiding them through the labyrinth of shifting time.

As they approached the heart of the Realm of Relativity, they encountered a massive black hole, its gravitational pull warping the space around it. The black hole was both a challenge and an opportunity.

"We need to use the black hole's gravity to our advantage," Alara said, her voice steady. "If we can get close enough without being pulled in, we can use its gravity to bend time and space, creating a shortcut to the next portal."

Leo nodded. "It's risky, but it's our best chance."

They approached the black hole cautiously, feeling the immense gravitational pull. Alara held the Chrono Crystal tightly, using its power to shield them from the worst of the gravitational forces.

As they neared the event horizon, the boundary beyond which nothing can escape the black hole's pull, they felt time stretching and bending around them. Alara focused all her strength, using the crystal to create a temporal bridge that would carry them across.

With a surge of energy, they crossed the event horizon, feeling the intense gravitational forces warp the very fabric of space-time. But the temporal bridge held, and they emerged on the other side, where the portal to the next realm awaited.

"We did it," Alara said, her voice filled with relief and triumph. "We used the black hole's gravity to bend time and space."

Seraphina's voice echoed with pride. "You have mastered the Realm of Relativity. Your understanding of time and space will serve you well in the battles ahead."

With a sense of accomplishment, they stepped through the portal, ready to face the next challenge. They knew that their journey was far from over, but they were stronger and more determined than ever.

As they emerged in a new realm, Alara felt a deep sense of purpose. They were not just guardians of time; they were explorers, scientists, and warriors, ready to face any challenge that lay ahead.

And as they looked to the future, they knew that them understanding of the laws of physics and the power of the Chrono Crystal would guide them on their journey, ensuring that history unfolded as it was meant to.

Alara stood at the edge of the ancient portal, the glow of the Nexus swirling beneath her feet like an untamed ocean of possibilities.

She took a deep breath, knowing that every choice she made would ripple across time. It wasn't just about herself or Leo anymore—it was about everyone. The weight of the decision loomed over her like a shadow, growing heavier with every second.

Yet, for the first time, she didn't feel alone. Leo stood beside her, his eyes locked onto hers with an intensity that seemed to transcend words. The bond between them was undeniable, forged through shared pain and the understanding that they were tied to something far greater than themselves. She wanted to speak, to voice her fears, but the moment felt too fragile for words. Instead, she held out her hand, and Leo took it, his grip firm and reassuring.

A sudden shift in the air, like a distant echo from the future, made Alara pause. She glanced at the Nexus. The crystalline structure hummed faintly, as if acknowledging her presence. The threads of time twisted and shimmered, waiting for her to make the choice. The future she feared seemed so close, and yet, there was a path forward. A path only she could decide.

"Whatever happens," Leo whispered, "we face it together."

Alara nodded, her resolve strengthening. The power of the Nexus pulsed beneath them, but it was the unity between her and Leo that gave her the courage to step forward into the unknown.

Chapter 4
Chrono Nexus

Opening:

The Chrono Nexus was not just a place—it was an entity, alive in ways that Alara could barely comprehend. As she stepped through the ancient archway, a wave of energy surged through her, making her hair stand on end. The air here was different, thicker, almost tangible. Every breath she took felt like it was being pulled from her lungs by the very fabric of time.

The others followed, their expressions a mix of awe and fear. The Nexus had a way of warping reality, twisting time and space in ways that defied logic. It was as though they were stepping into a world where every moment from the past, present, and future existed simultaneously.

Alara felt the weight of the Chrono Crystal pulsing in her hand as she and her allies stood at the threshold of the Chrono Nexus. The air was thick with anticipation, the kind that crackled like static electricity before a storm. They had faced many challenges, but nothing had prepared them for the mysteries and dangers that lay ahead.

"We've come this far," Leo said, adjusting his glasses and looking into Alara's eyes with unwavering support. "We can't turn back now."

Eamon, ever the stoic leader, nodded. "Remember, the Chrono Nexus holds the answers we seek. But it will also test us in ways we cannot yet imagine."

As they stepped through the shimmering portal, the world around them dissolved into a swirl of colours and lights, a dizzying array of sights and sounds that made Alara's heart race. When they finally emerged, they found themselves in a vast, otherworldly landscape where the rules of time and space seemed to bend and twist.

Arrival and Initial Exploration

The sky above them was a swirling vortex of colours, and the ground beneath their feet shifted and changed with every step. Strange structures and ancient ruins dotted the landscape, each one pulsing with a faint, otherworldly glow.

Leo was the first to speak. "This place... it's like nothing I've ever seen before. It's beautiful and terrifying all at once."

Alara nodded, her eyes scanning the horizon. "We need to be careful. The Chrono Nexus is not just a place; it's a living entity. It will react to our presence."

As they began to explore, they encountered phenomena that defied logic. Pockets of slowed and accelerated time, gravity wells that pulled and twisted their perceptions, and reflections that showed glimpses of their past and future.

They ventured deeper into the Nexus, passing through corridors that seemed to stretch on forever. The walls were adorned with symbols and glyphs that pulsed with a faint light, shifting and changing as they walked. Alara could feel the weight of history pressing down on her, as though every step she took was being watched by the eyes of those who had come before her.

"This place... it's like it's alive," Leo whispered, his voice barely audible in the oppressive silence.

"It is," Alara replied, her eyes scanning the shifting walls. "The Nexus isn't just a structure—it's a conduit. It connects us to every moment in time, past, present, and future. It's a living entity, shaped by the flow of time itself."

The ancient temple loomed ahead, its entrance marked by symbols that flickered with the faintest glow of time's forgotten secrets. As they entered, the group found themselves faced with the Temporal Labyrinth, a maze not just of space but of moments. Each turn presented not a new path but a new era—glimpses into both the past and future. Alara's mind raced as she realized the maze wasn't just a test of navigation, but of understanding time itself.Their journey led them to a massive structure at the heart of the Nexus, an ancient temple that seemed to pulse with the very essence of time. At the entrance, they found an inscription that spoke of a "Temporal Labyrinth," a maze that would test their understanding of time and their ability to manipulate it.

Eamon read the inscription aloud. "Only those who understand the true nature of time may pass. The Temporal Labyrinth will reveal your greatest strengths and deepest fears."

Alara felt a shiver run down her spine. "We have no choice. We need to find the heart of the Nexus and unlock its secrets."

As they entered the labyrinth, they found themselves in a maze of twisting corridors and shifting walls. Each turn took them deeper into the heart of the Nexus, and the challenges they faced became increasingly difficult.

As they moved deeper into the heart of the Nexus, they came upon a massive chamber, its ceiling so high that it disappeared into darkness. In the center of the room stood a towering structure—a monolith of crystal and metal, glowing with an otherworldly light. This was the core of the Nexus, the source of its power.

Alara stepped forward, her hand outstretched as though drawn to the structure by an invisible force. The crystal in her visions had led her here, to this moment. She could feel its energy pulsing through the room, resonating with something deep inside her.

"The crystal… it's here," she whispered, her voice barely above a breath.

The first test was a series of puzzles that required them to manipulate time to solve. Alara used the Chrono Crystal to slow down time, allowing Leo to decipher ancient scripts and Eamon to move objects with precision. They worked together seamlessly, their bond growing stronger with each challenge.

But the second test was far more personal. Each of them was confronted with visions of their past, moments of regret and pain that had shaped who they were. For Alara, it was the day she discovered her powers and the loss of her grandmother. For Leo, it was the moment he realized he was different from others and the isolation that followed. For Eamon, it was the battle that had cost him his family and the vow of vengeance he had taken.

These visions were not just memories; they were living, breathing entities that they had to confront and overcome. The emotional toll was immense, but it also brought them closer together.

But as she reached for the crystal, a sudden shockwave of energy burst from the monolith, sending her sprawling to the ground. The air crackled with electricity, and the walls of the chamber began to shimmer and shift, the very fabric of time warping around them.

"Alara!" Leo shouted, rushing to her side. He pulled her to her feet, his eyes wide with fear. "What's happening?"

Before she could answer, the air in the chamber rippled, and a figure appeared—Veridian. His presence sent a chill through Alara's spine. He had found them.As they emerged from the second test, Alara and Leo found themselves alone in a secluded part of the labyrinth. The air buzzed with unspoken feelings, a tension so palpable it seemed to hum. For a moment, the weight of their mission lifted, replaced by the simple, profound connection between them.

"Alara," Leo said softly, reaching out to take her hand. "I don't know what the future holds, but I want you to know that I'll always be by your side."

Alara felt her heart swell with emotion. "Leo, you've always been there for me. I don't know what I'd do without you."

In that moment, the world around them seemed to fade away, and they shared a kiss that was filled with the promise of a future together. It wasa moment of respite amid their journey, but it gave them the strength to carry on.

The final test of the Temporal Labyrinth was the most challenging yet. They found themselves in a vast chamber filled with floating platforms and swirling energy. At the centre of the chamber was a pedestal, upon which rested a glowing artifact that pulsed with the power of the Chrono Nexus.

Seraphina appeared before them; her presence more tangible than ever. "This is the Temporal Heart, the source of the Nexus's power. To claim it, you must demonstrate your mastery of time and your commitment to protecting the timeline."

The test required them to work together, using their combined strengths to manipulate time and navigate the platforms. It was a test of trust and unity, and they faced it with unwavering determination.

As they reached the pedestal, Alara placed the Chrono Crystal beside the Temporal Heart. A wave of energy surged through the chamber, and the Nexus came alive with light and power.

"You have proven yourselves worthy," Seraphina said, her voice filled with pride. "The Chrono Nexus is now under your protection. But be warned, the Timekeepers will not rest until they control it. You must be vigilant."

No sooner had Seraphina spoken than the chamber was filled with the dark presence of the Timekeepers. Their leader, a figure cloaked in shadows, stepped forward, his eyes glowing with malevolent intent.

"You may have unlocked the Nexus's power, but it belongs to us," the leader hissed. "We will control the timeline and reshape history as we see fit."

A fierce battle erupted, Alara and her allies clashing valiantly against the relentless Timekeepers. The air crackled with raw energy, spells, and weapons meeting in a symphony of chaos. Each side fought with unwavering determination, the fate of the timeline hanging in the balance.

During the chaos, Alara felt a surge of power from the Chrono Crystal. She realized that the key to defeating the Timekeepers lay in their connection to the timeline and their understanding of its true nature.

Using the combined power of the crystal and the Temporal Heart, Alara created a barrier that deflected the Timekeepers' attacks and began to unravel their control over time. The leader of the Timekeepers, realizing his defeat, made one last desperate attempt to seize the crystal, but Alara was ready.

With a final surge of energy, she unleashed a wave of temporal force that engulfed the leader, disintegrating his form and breaking the Timekeepers' hold on the Nexus.

As the energy faded, the chamber fell silent. The Timekeepers had been defeated, and the Chrono Nexus was secure.

Seraphina stepped forward; her eyes filled with gratitude. "You have proven yourselves true guardians of time. The future is in your hands."

With the Chrono Crystal and the Temporal Heart secured, Alara and her allies returned to the Nexus, their mission complete. They had faced incredible challenges and emerged stronger; their bond unbreakable.

As they stood together, gazing at the swirling energy of the Nexus, Alara felt a sense of peace. The journey had been long and arduous, but they

had succeeded. They had protected the timeline and ensured that history would unfold as it was meant to.

And as they looked to the future, they knew that whatever challenges lay ahead, they would face them together, as guardians of time.

Blurb:

In a world where time and space bend to the will of the powerful Chrono Nexus, Alara and her allies navigate a labyrinth of ancient mysteries, confronting their deepest fears. With the timeline's fate hanging in the balance, they face the ultimate test of strength, unity, and understanding. As romance blossoms and secrets unravel, they must protect the Nexus from the malevolent Timekeepers and secure the future. "Beyond Time's Veil" is a thrilling journey of love, adventure, and discovery that will leave readers breathless and yearning for more.

Synopsis:

Alara, Leo, and Eamon, armed with the Chrono Crystal, venture into the enigmatic Chrono Nexus, where the laws of time and space are fluid and ever-changing. Guided by the wise guardian Seraphina, they navigate the Temporal Labyrinth, confronting puzzles that test their understanding of optics and relativity, and personal trials that reveal their deepest fears and regrets. As romance blooms between Alara and Leo, their bond strengthens, giving them the resolve to face the challenges ahead.

Their journey leads them to the heart of the Nexus, where they unlock the power of the Temporal Heart, but their victory is short-lived as the Timekeepers launch a final assault. In a climactic battle filled with tension and energy, Alara and her allies use their mastery of time to defeat the Timekeepers and secure the Nexus. As guardians of time, they stand united, ready to face the future together.

The next day, Alara and Leo returned to Tempus Relics, eager to learn more. The elderly man greeted them with his knowing smile. "I see you are determined," he said. "The path to the Chrono Crystal is not an easy one. Many have tried and failed." Alara and Leo exchanged a determined glance. "We're ready," Alara said. The man nodded, pulling out an ancient map. "This will guide you to the crystal, but beware, the journey is fraught with danger."

As they secured the Chrono Nexus, Alara and her allies felt a moment of relief. But the tranquillity was short-lived. The ground beneath them trembled, and a new portal opened, swirling with a dark, ominous energy.

"What's happening?" Leo asked, his voice tinged with concern.

Seraphina's expression grew serious. "The Nexus is reacting to a disturbance in the timeline. Something or someone is trying to alter a crucial event."

Alara tightened her grip on the Chrono Crystal. "We need to stop it. Whatever it is, it can't be good."

They stepped through the portal, emerging in a desolate landscape where the sky was a tumultuous mix of dark clouds and lightning. In the distance, they saw a towering structure, pulsing with a malevolent energy.

"That's where we need to go," Eamon said, his voice resolute.

As they made their way towards the structure, they encountered strange anomalies—time loops that trapped them in endless cycles, and temporal echoes that played out scenes from their past. Each step was a battle against the forces trying to keep them from their goal.

In one of these temporal echoes, Alara found herself back in the moment when she first discovered her powers. She saw her younger self, scared, and confused, as her grandmother gently guided her.

"Trust in yourself, Alara," her grandmother's voice echoed. "You have a gift. Use it wisely."

The memory filled Alara with renewed determination. She had come a long way since that day, and she was ready to face whatever challenges lay ahead.

As they approached the towering structure, they discovered a hidden entrance leading to a secret chamber. The walls of the chamber were lined with ancient texts and scientific instruments, hinting at the advanced knowledge of the Nexus's creators.

Leo's eyes widened with excitement. "This is incredible. The technology here is centuries ahead of anything we've ever seen."

Alara felt a strange pull towards the centre of the chamber, where a pedestal held a small, intricately designed device. It seemed to hum with a life of its own.

"That's the Temporal Regulator," Seraphina said. "It controls the flow of time within the Nexus. If the Timekeepers get their hands on it, they could rewrite history."

As Alara reached for the device, the chamber was suddenly flooded with a blinding light. When the light faded, they found themselves in a different place—a lush, vibrant forest filled with strange, bioluminescent plants and creatures.

"This must be another layer of the Nexus," Leo said, looking around in awe.

They followed a winding path through the forest, the air filled with the sound of rustling leaves and distant animal calls. As they walked, Alara and Leo found themselves drifting away from the group, drawn to a secluded clearing by an unseen force.

In the clearing, they found a small, crystalline pool, its surface shimmering with an ethereal light. The atmosphere was serene and magical, a stark contrast to the challenges they had faced.

"Leo," Alara said softly, taking his hand. "I don't know what the future holds, but I know that I want to face it with you."

Leo looked into her eyes; his expression filled with emotion. "Alara, you've always been my anchor, my guiding star. I love you."

As they shared a tender kiss, the world around them seemed to fade away, leaving only the two of them and the love they shared. It was a moment of pure, unadulterated joy, a respite from the chaos that had surrounded them.

Their moment of peace was shattered by a sudden, violent tremor. The ground split open, and dark figures emerged from the shadows—the Timekeepers had found them.

"Get away from the Regulator!" the leader of the Timekeepers shouted; his voice filled with malice.

Alara and Leo sprang into action, their love for each other fuelling their determination to protect the Temporal Regulator. The air crackled with energy as they faced off against the Timekeepers, each side fighting with everything they had.

Amid the battle, Alara felt a surge of power from the Chrono Crystal. She realized that the key to defeating the Timekeepers lay in their connection to the timeline and them understanding of its true nature.

"Leo, focus on the crystal with me," Alara said, her voice steady despite the chaos around them. "We can use our bond to amplify its power."

Leo nodded; his eyes filled with determination. "Together."

They held the Chrono Crystal between them, channelling their love and connection into its core. The crystal pulsed with a brilliant light, and a wave of temporal energy surged through the clearing, engulfing the Timekeepers.

The leader of the Timekeepers, realizing his defeat, made one last desperate attempt to seize the Regulator, but Alara and Leo were ready. With a final surge of energy, they unleashed a powerful blast that disintegrated the leader and sent the remaining Timekeepers fleeing into the shadows.

As the dust settled, Alara and Leo stood together, the Temporal Regulator safe in their hands. They had faced incredible odds and emerged victorious, their love and determination guiding them through the darkest moments.

With the Temporal Regulator secured, Alara and her allies returned to the Nexus. Seraphina greeted them with a look of pride and relief.

"You have done well," she said. "The Nexus is safe, thanks to your bravery and your bond."

Alara nodded, her heart filled with gratitude. "We couldn't have done it without each other."

Seraphina gestured to the Temporal Regulator. "This device holds the key to understanding the true nature of time. It is a gift, but also a responsibility. Use it wisely."

As they studied the Regulator, they discovered that it contained a wealth of knowledge about the universe and the nature of time itself. They spent days poring over the texts and data, learning about advanced technologies and scientific principles that could change the world.

Alara and Leo, their bond stronger than ever, worked together to unlock the secrets of the Regulator. They discovered new ways to harness the power of the Chrono Crystal, using it to protect the timeline and ensure that history unfolded as it was meant to.

Epilogue: The Legacy of Love and Time

Years passed, and Alara and Leo continued to protect the Nexus, their love guiding them through every challenge. They built a life together, surrounded by friends and allies who shared their commitment to safeguarding the timeline.

Their story became a legend, a tale of love, bravery, and the power of thehuman spirit. The Chrono Nexus stood as a testament to their legacy, a beacon of hope and knowledge for future generations.

As they stood together, gazing at the swirling energy of the Nexus, Alara and Leo knew that their journey was far from over. But they faced the future with confidence, knowing that they had each other and the power of love to guide them.

And as they looked to the horizon, they knew that the promise of adventure and discovery would always be a part of their lives, a reminder that the power of time and love could conquer any obstacle.

The success of securing the Temporal Regulator was short-lived. The Nexus, although temporarily at peace, began to show signs of instability. Alara and Leo, both intensely focused on their mission, found themselvesin conflict more often than not.

Alara, driven by the responsibility of the Chrono Crystal and the knowledge they had gained, pushed herself and the team to the limits. Her relentless determination sometimes came off as harsh, especially to Leo, who had always been the voice of reason and caution.

"Alara, you need to rest," Leo said one evening as they poured over ancient texts in the Nexus's library. "You're pushing too hard. We all need a break."

"There's no time for rest, Leo," Alara snapped, her eyes filled with afiery intensity. "The Nexus is unstable, and the Timekeepers are still out there. We can't afford to relax."

Leo's frustration boiled over. "This isn't just about the mission, Alara. You're shutting me out. We're supposed to be a team."

Alara turned away, her voice trembling with a mix of anger and exhaustion. "Maybe I need to do this on my own."

The tension between them grew, creating a rift that threatened to tear them apart. The pressure of their mission, combined with their personal struggles, made the atmosphere within the Nexus charged with unresolved emotions.

In the midst of their conflict, they discovered hidden texts within the Nexus's library that hinted at a greater danger. The Timekeepers were not just after the Chrono Crystal; they sought to rewrite history entirely, erasing key events that shaped the future.

The texts spoke of a device called the Chrono Rewriter, capable of altering the timeline on a massive scale. It was hidden deep within the Nexus, protected by layers of temporal defences.

"We need to find the Chrono Rewriter before the Timekeepers do," Eamon said, his voice filled with urgency. "If they get their hands on it, they could change everything."

Alara and Leo, despite their personal differences, knew the gravity of the situation. They had to put aside their conflict and work together to prevent the Timekeepers from succeeding.

Their search led them to the deepest, most treacherous parts of the Nexus. The environment became increasingly hostile, with temporal storms that threatened to tear them apart and gravity wells that distorted their perceptions.

As they navigated these dangers, Alara and Leo were forced to confront their unresolved feelings. The stress of their mission had brought their insecurities and fears to the surface, but it also made them realize how much they needed each other.

One night, as they camped in a small cave to escape a temporal storm, Leo broke the silence. "Alara, I'm sorry for what I said. I didn't mean to push you away. I just... I care about you, and I don't want to lose you."

Alara's eyes softened, tears welling up as she looked at him. "I'm sorry too, Leo. I've been so focused on the mission that I forgot what's really important. You're right. We are a team, and I can't do this without you."

Their reconciliation was heartfelt and emotional, rekindling their bond and reminding them of the love that had brought them together. They shared a tender kiss, sealing their commitment to each other and their mission.

As they continued their journey, Alara and Leo found themselves in a beautiful, serene part of the Nexus. It was a lush, enchanted forest with bioluminescent flowers that glowed softly in the moonlight. The air was filled with the sweet scent of blooming jasmine, and the gentle hum of the forest created a peaceful, magical atmosphere.

In the heart of the forest, they found a clear lake, its surface reflecting the starry sky above. Alara and Leo sat by the lake, holding hands, and gazing at the beauty around them.

"Leo, I've never seen anything so beautiful," Alara whispered, restingher head on his shoulder.

Leo smiled, his heart swelling with love. "It's like a dream. And being here with you makes it perfect."

As they sat there, the love they shared deepened, transcending the challenges they faced. The universe seemed to align, bringing them closer than ever. They made a promise to each other, a vow of love and commitment that would carry them through whatever lay ahead.

Their moment of peace was abruptly shattered when they heard a commotion nearby. They rushed to the source of the noise and found a group of Timekeepers attempting to activate the Chrono Rewriter. The device was a complex array of gears and crystals, glowing with anominous light.

"Stop them!" Eamon shouted, drawing his weapon.

A fierce battle ensued, with Alara, Leo, and their allies fighting desperately to prevent the Timekeepers from activating the device. The air crackled with energy as spells and weapons clashed, each side fighting with everything they had.

In the heat of the battle, Alara realized that the only way to stop the Timekeepers was to use the Chrono Crystal to disrupt the Rewriter's power source. She and Leo moved as one, their connection and love guiding them through the chaos.

"Leo, we need to do this together," Alara said, her voice filled with determination.

Leo nodded, his eyes meeting hers. "I'm with you, Alara. Always."

Together, they channelled their combined energy into the Chrono Crystal, creating a powerful surge that destabilized the Chrono Rewriter. The device began to glow brighter and brighter, its energy reaching a critical point.

"Now!" Alara shouted.

With a final burst of power, they unleashed a wave of temporal energy that engulfed the Rewriter, disintegrating it and the Timekeepers in a brilliant explosion of light.

As the dust settled, Alara and Leo stood together, breathless but victorious. The Chrono Nexus had been saved, and the timeline was secure once more.

Seraphina appeared before them, her expression filled with pride and gratitude. "You have done it. The Nexus is safe, thanks to your bravery and your bond."

Alara nodded, her heart swelling with emotion. "We couldn't have done it without each other."

Eamon stepped forward; his face serious but relieved. "We've faced incredible challenges, but we've emerged stronger. We are guardians of time, and we will continue to protect the Nexus and the timeline."

Epilogue: A New Beginning With the Chrono Rewriter destroyed and the Timekeepers defeated, Alara and her allies returned to their home world. They had faced unimaginable dangers and emerged victorious; their bond stronger than ever.

Alara and Leo built a life together, their love a guiding light that carried them through every challenge. They continued to protect the timeline, using the knowledge and power they had gained to ensure that history unfolded as it was meant to.

Their story became a legend, a tale of love, bravery, and the power of the human spirit. The Chrono Nexus stood as a testament to their legacy, a beacon of hope and knowledge for future generations.

As they stood together, gazing at the swirling energy of the Nexus, Alara and Leo knew that their journey was far from over. But they faced the future with confidence, knowing that they had each other and the power of love to guide them.

And as they looked to the horizon, they knew that the promise of adventure and discovery would always be a part of their lives, a reminder that the power of time and love could conquer any obstacle.

Chapter - 5
The Timekeepers

The tranquillity that had settled over the Chrono Nexus was shattered by a sudden, chilling realization. As Alara, Leo, and their allies began to delve deeper into the mysteries of the Temporal Regulator, they discovered an ominous message hidden within the ancient texts.

Alara was the first to notice the strange symbols, hidden within the intricate diagrams and calculations. "These aren't just instructions," she murmured, tracing her fingers over the faded ink. "They're warnings."

Leo peered over her shoulder, his brow furrowing. "Warnings about what?"

Eamon, standing nearby, looked grave. "It seems the Timekeepers had a contingency plan. If their main forces failed, they would activate a sleeper cell—agents embedded within the fabric of time itself, ready to strike at a moment's notice."

The air grew tense as the implications of this revelation sank in. The Timekeepers weren't defeated; they were lying in wait, poised to unleash chaos upon the timeline.

As if on cue, the ground beneath them trembled. A deep, resonant hum filled the air, and the walls of the Nexus shimmered with an eerie light. Alara's heart pounded in her chest. "They're activating the sleeper cell."

Suddenly, dark figures began to materialize around them—Timekeepers, their eyes glowing with an otherworldly light. These were not the ragged remnants they had fought before; these were elite operatives, their presence exuding power and menace.

Leo stepped forward, his voice steady despite the fear gripping his heart. "We need to act fast. If they gain control of the Nexus, all our efforts willbe for nothing."

Eamon drew his weapon, his expression fierce. "Then we fight. Weprotect the Nexus at all costs."

The ensuing battle was unlike anything they had faced before. The Timekeepers moved with deadly precision, their attacks synchronized and relentless. Alara and Leo fought side by side, their bond strengthening their resolve.

Alara used the Chrono Crystal to manipulate time, creating

temporal shields and slowing their enemies. Leo's quick thinking and sharp reflexes complemented her abilities, together forming an impenetrable defence.

But the Timekeepers were formidable, their mastery of time rivalling their own. Eamon was locked in combat with one of the leaders, their swords clashing in a deadly dance. "We can't hold them off forever!" he shouted; his voice strained with effort.

In the midst of the chaos, Alara spotted something—a faint, pulsing glow emanating from the centre of the Nexus. It was the Temporal Core, the heart of the Nexus's power. If they could reach it, they might be able to turn the tide of the battle.

"Leo, we need to get to the Temporal Core!" Alara yelled, deflecting an attack with a sweep of her arm.

Leo nodded, his eyes meeting hers with unwavering trust. "Let's go."

They fought their way through the throng of enemies, each step bringing them closer to the core. The energy in the air was palpable, the very fabric of time seeming to ripple around them.

As they reached the core, Alara felt a surge of power from the Chrono Crystal. "We can use this," she said, her voice

filled with a mix of hope and determination. "We can amplify the crystal's power through the core and create a temporal wave that will disable the Timekeepers."

Leo's eyes widened with realization. "But it could also destabilize the entire Nexus."

Alara's gaze was steady. "It's a risk we have to take. It's our only chance."

With Leo's help, Alara positioned the Chrono Crystal at the centre of the core. They could feel the energy building, a powerful force that threatened to overwhelm them. The Timekeepers, sensing their plan, redoubled their efforts, but Eamon and the others held them at bay with a desperate ferocity.

"Now!" Alara shouted, her voice echoing through the chamber.

They activated the core, and a blinding light filled the Nexus. The temporal wave surged outward, a cascade of energy that swept through the Timekeepers, freezing them in place and unravelling their control over time.

For a moment, it seemed as if the entire Nexus was tearing apart at the seams. But then, slowly, the energy began to stabilize. The light dimmed, and the hum of the Nexus returned to its normal, steady rhythm.

As the dust settled, Alara and Leo stood together, their breaths coming in ragged gasps. The Timekeepers lay immobilized, their plans thwarted.

Eamon approached, his expression a mixture of relief and admiration. "You did it. You saved the Nexus."

Alara nodded, her heart still pounding. "We did it. Together."

Seraphina appeared, her ethereal form glowing with approval. "You have proven your worth once again. The Nexus is safe, thanks to your courage and ingenuity."

But Alara knew that their journey was far from over. The threat of the Timekeepers had been neutralized, but the timeline remained fragile, and the responsibility of safeguarding it weighed heavily on her shoulders.

In the days that followed, Alara, Leo, and their allies worked tirelessly to repair the damage done to the Nexus. They fortified its defences and strengthened their understanding of the temporal energies that flowed through it.

Through it all, Alara and Leo's bond grew stronger. They had faced unimaginable dangers and come through the other side, their love and trust in each other unshakable.

One evening, as they stood at the entrance of the Nexus, gazing out at the swirling energies that represented the vast, interconnected web of time, Leo took Alara's hand in his.

"We've been through so much," he said softly. "But I know that as long as we're together, we can face anything."

Alara smiled, her heart filled with warmth and hope. "We are stronger together. And whatever the future holds, we'll face it side by side."

As they stood there, united in their resolve, they knew that their journey was far from over. The timeline was a living, breathing entity, filled with endless possibilities and challenges. But they were ready to face it, together.

And as they looked to the horizon, they knew that the promise of adventure and discovery would always be a part of their lives, a reminder that the power of love and time could conquer any obstacle.

Chapter - 6
The First Encounter

After their triumph over the Timekeepers, Alara, Leo, and their allies spent several weeks fortifying the Chrono Nexus and restoring balance to the timeline. The sense of victory was sweet, but a lingering unease settled over them. They knew their journey was far from over, and the threats to the timeline could come from anywhere and at any time.

One evening, as the group gathered around a campfire near the heart of the Nexus, Seraphina shared a vision she had experienced. "I've seen a shadow moving through time," she said, her voice heavy with concern. "A powerful entity that we have yet to face."

Eamon, ever the warrior, leaned forward. "Who or what is it?"

Seraphina shook her head. "I do not know. But its presence is unlike anything we have encountered. It's as if time itself bends to its will."

Alara exchanged a glance with Leo, her heart pounding with a mix of fear and curiosity. "We need to be prepared for anything."

The next day, as they continued their work, a strange phenomenon occurred. A portal opened within the Nexus, but it was unlike any they had seen before. The edges shimmered with a dark, almost sinister energy, and the air around it crackled with tension.

Leo, with his keen eye for detail, immediately sensed the danger. "This isn't one of our portals," he said, his voice tight. "Something—or someone—has forced their way in."

The group gathered, weapons at the ready, as the portal stabilized. From within the swirling darkness, a figure emerged. Tall and imposing, with an aura of power that seemed to distort the very fabric of reality around them.

"Who are you?" Alara demanded, stepping forward with the Chrono Crystal in hand.

The figure's eyes glowed with an unsettling light as they spoke. "I am Veridian, Master of the Temporal Void. And I have come to claim whatis mine."

Veridian's presence was overwhelming. The air seemed to grow heavy, and a palpable sense of dread filled the Nexus. Alara and Leo exchanged a quick glance, their resolve hardening.

"You have no claim here," Eamon said, his voice steady despite the tension. "This Nexus is under our protection."

Veridian laughed, a sound that echoed through the chamber like a dark melody. "You protect what you do not understand. The power of the Nexus is beyond your comprehension."

With a swift motion, Veridian's power warped reality itself—time buckled and screamed as the world twisted, his energy engulfing them in an unforgiving wave of chaos, sending the group sprawling. Alara managed to raise a shield in time to deflect the worst of the blast, but the force of the attack was staggering.

"We have to work together," Leo shouted, helping Alara to her feet. "Combine our powers!"

Alara nodded, her determination blazing. Together, they channelled their energy into the Chrono Crystal, creating a barrier to shield them from Veridian's attacks. But the Master of the Temporal Void was relentless, and his control over time seemed absolute.

As the battle raged, Veridian demonstrated his mastery over the Temporal Void. He manipulated the flow of time with ease, creating illusions and temporal traps that disoriented and confused his opponents.

At one point, Alara found herself facing a vision of her past—her grandmother, the day she discovered her powers, the moments of doubt and fear. But she quickly realized it was a trick, a manifestation of Veridian's power to unsettle her.

"You think you can distract me with these illusions?" she shouted, dispelling the vision with a wave of her hand. "I am stronger than that!"

Leo, too, faced his own trials. Veridian conjured a version of Leo's younger self, filled with insecurities and self-doubt. But Leo stood firm, his love for Alara and his commitment to their mission giving him the strength to resist.

"We will not be swayed by your tricks," Leo declared, his voice ringing with conviction. "We are united, and our bond is stronger than your darkness."

Realizing brute force alone would not suffice, Veridian changed tactics. He began to speak, his voice smooth and persuasive. "You seek to protect the timeline, but do you utterly understand its potential? The Nexus holds the key to rewriting history, to erasing mistakes and creating a perfect world."

Alara's eyes narrowed. "What are you suggesting?" Veridian's expression softened, almost paternal. "Join me.

Together, we can harness the power of the Nexus to reshape time itself. Imagine a world without suffering, without war. A world where you control the destiny of humanity."

For a moment, doubt flickered in Alara's mind. The idea was tempting—so much pain and loss could be prevented. But then she remembered the lessons her grandmother had taught her about the dangers of absolute power.

"You speak of control, but what you offer is tyranny," Alara replied, her voice resolute. "We do not have the right to rewrite history to suit our desires."

Leo stepped forward; his gaze unwavering. "We protect the timeline because it is a gift, not a tool for manipulation. Your vision is a perversion of that gift."

Veridian's eyes flashed with anger. "Fools! You cannot comprehend the power you reject."

He launched another attack, but this time, Alara and Leo were ready. They combined their energies, channelling the power of the ChronoCrystal with a precision born of their deep connection and mutual trust.

The chamber was filled with a brilliant light as their combined power clashed with Veridian's dark energy. The ground shook, and the very air seemed to vibrate with the intensity of their battle.

At the critical moment, Alara and Leo unleashed a focused beam of temporal energy, striking Veridian and shattering his control over the Temporal Void. With a scream of rage, Veridian was forced back through the portal, which closed behind him with a final, resounding boom.

The silence that followed was almost deafening. The group stood together, their breaths coming in ragged gasps. The battle had beenfierce, and the toll was evident in their tired expressions.

"We did it," Eamon said, his voice filled with relief. "We drove him back."

Alara nodded, though her mind was still racing. "But he'll return. Veridian is too powerful to be defeated so easily. We need to be preparedfor when he comes back."

Leo placed a comforting hand on her shoulder. "We will be. Together, we're stronger than he can ever be."

Seraphina appeared, her ethereal form glowing with approval. "You havefaced a great challenge and emerged victorious. But the road ahead is long, and the threats to the timeline are many."

Alara took a deep breath, feeling the weight of their responsibility settle over her once more. "We will continue to protect the Nexus and the timeline. No matter what comes our way."

That night, as the group rested, Alara and Leo found themselves alone by the campfire. The stars above seemed to shine with a renewed brilliance, a reminder of the vastness of the universe and the intricate web of time they were sworn to protect.

"Leo," Alara said softly, her eyes reflecting the flickering flames. "Today was a narrow escape. I realized how much I rely on you, how much your presence gives me strength."

Leo smiled, his hand gently clasping hers. "We've been through so much together, Alara. Our bond is what makes us strong. As long as we're together, we can face anything."

Alara leaned into him, finding comfort in his warmth. "I know. And I'm grateful for every moment we have."

They sat in silence for a while, watching the fire and feeling the serenity of the night. It was a rare moment of peace in the midst of their tumultuous journey, and they cherished it deeply.

The next morning, they began to plan for the future. The encounter with Veridian had shown them that the threats to the Nexus were more complex and dangerous than they had imagined. They needed to be ready for anything.

"We need to strengthen our defences," Eamon said, his tone decisive. "Veridian's power is formidable, and we can't afford to be caught off guard again."

Seraphina nodded in agreement. "We must also deepen our understanding of the Nexus's capabilities. There are secrets here that we have yet to uncover."

Alara and Leo took the lead in organizing their efforts. They divided tasks among the group, ensuring that everyone had a role to play in their ongoing mission. It was a daunting task, but their determination was unwavering.

As the days passed, they made considerable progress. The Nexus's defences were fortified, and their knowledge of temporal mechanics grew. They trained relentlessly, honing their skills, and preparing for the battles that lay ahead.

Through it all, the bond between Alara and Leo continued to grow. Their love was a source of strength and inspiration, a beacon of hope in the darkest of times.

One evening, as they stood together at the entrance of the Nexus, watching the swirling energies, Alara felt a sense of calm wash over her. "We've come so far, and we have so much more to do. But I believe in us, Leo. I believe in our ability to protect the timeline."

Just as they were beginning to settle into their new routines, a mysterious figure appeared at the edge of their camp. Tall and cloaked in shadows, the figure moved with a grace that suggested both strength and wisdom.

Eamon was the first to notice and called out, "Who goes there?"

The figure stepped forward, revealing a face that was both ancient and ageless. "I am Thalis, an ally in your fight to protect the timeline."

Alara's eyes narrowed with suspicion. "How do we know we can trust you?"

Thalis smiled, a gesture that seemed to hold centuries of knowledge. "Because I was once a guardian of the Nexus, long before your time. I have seen the rise and fall of many threats, and I have come to offer my assistance."

Seraphina nodded, recognizing the name. "Thalis was a legend among the guardians. His knowledge and experience could be invaluable."

Alara and Leo exchanged a glance, then Alara stepped forward and extended her hand. "Welcome, Thalis. We could use all the help we can get."

With Thalis' guidance, the group's training intensified. He taught them advanced techniques for manipulating time and space, revealing secrets that had been lost to the ages. Under his tutelage, their powers grew stronger and more refined.

Thalis also shared his knowledge of the Nexus's history, explaining its origins and the true extent of its power. "The Nexus is more than a gateway through time," he said one evening as they gathered around the campfire. "It is a living entity, connected to every moment that has ever existed. To protect it, you must understand it."

Alara listened intently, her mind racing with the possibilities. "If we can truly master the Nexus, we could prevent any future threats from arising."

Thalis nodded. "But remember, with great power comes great responsibility. The Nexus must be used wisely, for the good of all time."

Despite the looming threats, there were moments of peace and camaraderie. Alara and Leo's relationship continued to blossom, their love providing a beacon of hope for everyone.

One night, as they walked together under the starlit sky, Leo took Alara'shand. "I never imagined I'd find something so wonderful in the midst of all this chaos," he said softly.

Alara smiled, her heart swelling with love. "Neither did I. But I'm grateful for every moment we have together."

They paused by the edge of the Nexus, the swirling energies creating a mesmerizing display. "No matter what happens," Alara said, "we'll faceit together."

Leo nodded, his gaze steady and filled with determination. "Together, always."

Their peace was shattered one fateful morning when the Nexus wasattacked. A group of shadowy figures, more formidable and coordinated than any they had faced before, launched a surprise assault.

Eamon rallied the group, his voice commanding and strong. "Defend the Nexus! We cannot let them breach our defences!"

Alara and Leo fought side by side, their movements synchronized and fluid. Thalis, despite his age, moved with incredible speed and precision, his mastery of temporal energy on full display.

But the attackers were relentless, their tactics advanced and their determination unwavering. It quickly became clear that they were not just any group of enemies—they were agents of Veridian, sent to reclaimthe Nexus.

In the midst of the battle, Alara spotted a familiar figure among the attackers. It was one of the Timekeepers they had defeated before, now returned vigorously.

"We need to end this, now," Alara shouted to Leo, her voice filled with urgency.

Leo nodded, his eyes blazing with determination. "Let's finish this."

Together, they channelled their energy into the Chrono Crystal, creating a powerful surge that swept through the battlefield. The attackers were thrown back, their ranks breaking under the force of the blast.

Thalis joined them, adding his power to theirs. "We must push them back through the portal. It's the only way to secure the Nexus."

With a combined effort, they forced the attackers towards the portal. The air crackled with energy as they unleashed a final, devastating wave, sending the enemies tumbling back into the temporal void.

As the portal closed behind them, silence fell over the Nexus. The battle was over, but the cost was high. They had won, but the threat of Veridianstill loomed.

In the aftermath, the group gathered to assess the damage and plan their next steps. Thalis' presence was a source of comfort and strength, his wisdom guiding their decisions.

"We need to be ready for whatever comes next," Eamon said, his voice steady. "Veridian will not stop until he has control of the Nexus."

Seraphina nodded in agreement. "We must strengthen our defences and continue to train. But we must also seek out allies. There are others who can help us in this fight."

Alara and Leo stood together, their resolve unwavering. "We will do whatever it takes to protect the timeline," Alara said, her voice filled with determination. "We will find allies, and we will stand against Veridian."

With renewed purpose, the group set out to seek allies. Thalis led them to ancient places of power, where they hoped to find those who would join their cause.

Their journey took them to distant lands and hidden realms, each step filled with danger and discovery. Along the way, they encountered beings of incredible power and wisdom, some willing to help, others more hesitant.

But through it all, Alara and Leo's bond remained strong. Their love was a source of strength and inspiration, a reminder of what they were fighting for.

As they journeyed, they began to gather a diverse group of allies—warriors, scholars, and beings of incredible power. Each brought their unique skills and knowledge, strengthening their cause.

One night, as they camped under the stars, Alara looked around at their growing group of allies. "We are not alone," she said softly. "We have the strength of many, and together, we will protect the timeline."

Leo smiled, his hand gently squeezing hers. "We are stronger together. And we will face whatever comes, side by side."

With their new allies, they returned to the Nexus, their spirits high. They spent days fortifying their defences and preparing for the battles ahead. The air was filled with a sense of anticipation and determination.

One evening, as they gathered around the campfire, Thalis shared a story from his past. "In all my years as a guardian, I have never seen a group as determined and united as you," he said, his voice filled with pride. "You have the strength and the heart to protect the timeline."

Alara and Leo exchanged a glance, their hearts swelling with pride and gratitude. "We will do whatever it takes," Alara said. "For the timeline, and for each other."

As they prepared for the next phase of their journey, a sense of foreboding settled over them. They knew that the battles ahead would be even more challenging, and the stakes higher than ever.

But they also knew that they had the strength of their allies and the power of their love to guide them. Together, they would face whatever came their way.

And as they stood at the entrance of the Nexus, gazing out at the swirling energies, they knew that their journey was far from over. The promise of adventure and discovery was still ahead, and they were ready to face it, side by side.

In the days that followed, they continued to train and prepare, their resolve unwavering. They knew that Veridian would return, and they needed to be ready.

But they also knew that they had the strength of their allies and the power of their love to guide them. Together, they would face whatever came their way.

And as they looked to the horizon, they knew that the promise of adventure and discovery would always be a part of their lives, a reminder that the power of time and love could conquer any obstacle.

Chapter - 7
Allies And Enemies

As they stood at the threshold of the unknown, Alara, Leo, and their allies knew that their greatest challenges were still ahead. The battle with Veridian had shown them the true extent of the threats they faced, but it had also revealed their own strength and resilience.

In the days to come, they would seek out new allies and confront old enemies, forging bonds that would shape the future of the timeline. The road ahead was uncertain, but their hearts were filled with hope and determination.

Together, they would protect the Nexus and the timeline, no matter the cost. For they were not just guardians of time; they were warriors of light, united by love and bound by destiny.

And as they stepped forward into the unknown, they knew that their journey was just beginning. The promise of adventure and discovery lay ahead, and they were ready to face it, side by side.

With Chapter 6, "The First Encounter," we have set the stage for the next phase of the story, introducing new allies, and foreshadowing the challenges to come. This chapter is designed to keep readers engaged and eager for the next instalment, "Allies and Enemies." If there are any specific elements or adjustments you'd like to include, please let me know!

The days following their encounter with Veridian were filled with a heavy tension that hung over the Nexus. Alara and Leo were both grappling with the weight of their responsibilities and the sacrifices they had to make. They worked tirelessly, often pushing themselves to the brink of exhaustion.

Alara noticed that Leo had been distant, his eyes often clouded with worry. She wanted to reach out to him, to comfort him, but she was dealing with her own fears and anxieties. They both hid their pain, not wanting to burden the other.

One evening, as they sat by the campfire, Leo's facade finally cracked. Alara noticed him wincing as he shifted his position, and she saw the dark circles under his eyes that spoke of sleepless nights.

"Leo are you okay?" she asked, her voice filled with concern. Leo forced a smile. "I'm fine, Alara. Just a bit tired, that's all."

But Alara wasn't convinced. She reached out and gently touched his hand. "You don't have to hide your pain from me.

We're in this together."

Leo sighed, the weight of his burdens finally surfacing. "It's just... everything feels so overwhelming. I'm scared, Alara. Scared that we won't be able to protect the Nexus, that we'll fail."

Alara's heart ached for him. She had been feeling the same fears but seeing them reflected in Leo's eyes made them all the more real. "I'm scared too," she admitted, her voice trembling. "But we have to stay strong. For each other, and for the Nexus."

That night, as they lay side by side in their tent, Alara could feel the walls they had both built around their hearts beginning to crumble. Leo reached out and took her hand, holding it tightly.

"Thank you, Alara," he whispered. "For being my strength."

Tears welled up in Alara's eyes. "And thank you, Leo. For being my light in the darkness."

They lay there in silence, their hands intertwined, finding comfort in each other's presence. For the first time in weeks, Alara felt a glimmer of hope. They had each other, and that was enough.

The next day, while exploring a hidden chamber in the Nexus, they stumbled upon an ancient manuscript. The pages were filled with cryptic symbols and diagrams, but one passage caught Alara's eye.

"It's a prophecy," she said, her voice tinged with excitement and fear. "A prophecy about the chosen ones who will protect the timeline."

Leo leaned in; his curiosity piqued. "What does it say?"

Alara read aloud, her voice steady. "The chosen ones will face great trials and tribulations, their hearts tested by fire. But through their pain and sacrifice, they will find the strength to protect the timeline and ensure the future of humanity."

Leo's eyes widened. "It's talking about us."

Alara nodded, her heart pounding. "We were meant to find this. It's a sign that we're on the right path."

As they delved deeper into the manuscript, they found passages that spoke of small gestures of love and kindness, acts that would strengthen their bond and give them the courage to face their trials.

Alara realized that despite their pain, she and Leo had been doing these things for each other all along. The way Leo always made sure she had food to eat, even when he wasn't hungry. The way Alara stayed up late to keep watch, allowing Leo to rest.

They had been each other's strength without even realizing it.

That evening, as they sat by the campfire once more, Alara decided to share her thoughts with Leo. "I think we've been following the prophecy without even knowing it," she said, her voice soft but filled with conviction.

Leo looked at her, his eyes filled with curiosity. "What do you mean?"

Alara took a deep breath. "All those trivial things we do for each other. Making sure we're okay, staying strong even when we're scared. Those are the gestures the prophecy talked about. We've been each other's strength all along."

Leo's eyes filled with tears. "I hadn't realized... Alara, you've been my rock. I don't know what I'd do without you."

Alara's heart swelled with love and gratitude. "And you've been my light, Leo. Together, we're unstoppable."

As the realization sank in, the weight of their hidden pain lifted. They held each other close, tears streaming down their faces. It was a cathartic release, a moment of vulnerability that brought them even closer.

"I'm sorry for hiding my pain from you," Leo whispered, his voice choked with emotion.

"And I'm sorry for doing the same," Alara replied, her tears mingling with his. "But we're stronger together, and we'll face whatever comes our way."

They sat there, holding each other, their hearts intertwined. The fire crackled softly, casting a warm glow over them. In that moment, they knew they could face anything as long as they had each other.

The next morning, they woke with a renewed sense of purpose. The prophecy had given them hope, a belief that they were destined to protect the timeline. They faced their training with a newfound Vigor, their bond stronger than ever.

As they worked, they exchanged small gestures of love and support. A reassuring touch, a shared smile, a whispered word of encouragement. These gestures, though small, made all the difference.

Thalis noticed the change in them and smiled. "You have found your strength in each other," he said, his voice filled with pride. "That is the greatest gift of all."

Alara and Leo exchanged a glance, their hearts swelling with love and gratitude. They had been through so much, but their journey was far fromover. They had each other, and that was enough.

Chapter - 8
The Hidden Truth

As they delved deeper into the mysteries of the Nexus, they uncovered more secrets and hidden truths. They learned of the great sacrifices made by those who came before them, and the immense power they now wielded.

But through it all, they never lost sight of the love and support they had found in each other. It was their greatest strength, the hidden truth that would carry them through even the darkest of times.

While exploring another section of the Nexus, Alara and Leo stumbled upon an ancient device known as the Temporal Beacon. This device, they discovered, could amplify the power of the Chrono Crystal, potentially giving them an edge in their fight against Veridian.

"This could change everything," Leo said, examining the intricate mechanisms of the Beacon. "With this, we might be able to turn the tide in our favour."

Alara nodded, her eyes filled with determination. "We need to learn how to use it. But we must be careful. Such power can be dangerous if not oversaw properly."

As they worked to understand the Temporal Beacon, Alara and Leo found themselves growing even closer. They shared their hopes and fears, their dreams, and doubts, finding solace in each other's presence.

One night, as they sat by the campfire, Leo looked at Alara, his eyes filled with a tender intensity. "Alara, no matter what happens,

I want you to know that I love you. You are my strength, my hope, my everything."

Tears filled Alara's eyes as she reached out and took his hand. "And I love you, Leo. Together, we are stronger than anything that comes our way. We will protect the Nexus and the timeline, no matter the cost."

With the Temporal Beacon now operational, Alara and Leo gathered their allies for one final briefing. Thalis, Seraphina, Eamon, and the others listened intently as Alara outlined their plan.

"We will use the Beacon to amplify the Chrono Crystal's power," she explained. "This will give us the strength to repel any attacks and secure the Nexus once and for all."

Eamon nodded, his expression resolute. "We are ready. Whatever comes, we will face it together."

Before embarking on their mission, Alara and Leo took a moment to themselves. They stood at the entrance of the Nexus, looking out at the swirling energies that represented the vast expanse of time.

"Are you ready?" Leo asked, his voice filled with a mix of determination and apprehension.

Alara took a deep breath, her heart pounding. "As ready as I will ever be. But no matter what happens, I know we will face it together."

Leo smiled, his eyes shining with love. "Together, always."

They embraced, their hearts beating as one. In that moment, they knew that their love and determination would see them through whatever trials lay ahead.

As they activated the Temporal Beacon, a brilliant light filled the Nexus. The energy from the Beacon surged through the Chrono Crystal, creating a protective shield around the Nexus.

But during this, Alara and Leo discovered something unexpected. Hidden within the Beacon's mechanisms was a message from the original guardians of the Nexus.

As Alara and Leo carefully examined the Temporal Beacon, they found a hidden compartment containing an ancient scroll. The scroll was delicate, its edges frayed with age, but the writing was still legible. Alara gently unrolled it, her eyes scanning the text.

"It's a message from the original guardians," she whispered, her voice filled with awe.

Leo leaned in, his curiosity piqued. "What does it say?"

Alara began to read aloud, her voice steady despite the tremor of excitement. "To the future guardians of the Nexus, know that you are not alone. The power of the Nexus is vast and can be both a blessing and a curse. Use it wisely, and remember that the true strength lies in the bonds you forge and the love you share. Trust in each other, and you will overcome any obstacle."

Leo's eyes softened as he listened. "They knew we would find this. They believed in us."

Alara nodded, her heart swelling with gratitude. "And we must honour their belief by continuing to protect the Nexus and the timeline."

With the message from the past guiding them, Alara and Leo prepared for what they knew would be their greatest test. The Temporal Beacon's activation had drawn the attention of powerful forces, and they could feel the weight of impending challenges pressing down on them.

Thalis gathered the group, his expression serious. "We have done all we can to prepare. Now, we must stand strong and face whatever comes our way. Remember the words of the guardians: trust in each other and the bonds you have forged."

As the group stood together, united in their resolve, Alara and Leo exchanged a glance filled with unspoken understanding. They had come so far and faced so much, but their journey was far from over.

Just as they were about to face their next challenge, a figure emerged from the shadows. It was a woman with an air of mystery and power, her eyes glowing with an otherworldly light.

"I am Lyra, a guardian of the astral plane," she announced, her voice echoing with authority. "I have watched over the Nexus for centuries, and I have come to aid you in your fight."

Alara and Leo exchanged a glance of cautious optimism. "Why now?" Leo asked, his voice tinged with suspicion.

Lyra's gaze softened. "Because I have seen the strength of your bond and the purity of your intentions. You are the guardians we have been waiting for."

With Lyra's arrival, the group felt a renewed sense of hope. Her knowledge of the astral plane and her ability to manipulate energy added a powerful new dimension to their efforts.

Together, they trained under Lyra's guidance, learning to harness the full potential of the Temporal Beacon. Alara and Leo found their abilities growing stronger, their connection deeper than ever before.

One night, as they practiced by the campfire, Lyra approached Alara. "You have a great gift, Alara. Your bond with Leo is your greatest strength. Never forget that."

Alara smiled, her heart filled with gratitude. "Thank you, Lyra. We will use our bond to protect the Nexus and the timeline."

As they continued their preparations, they discovered a hidden threat lurking within the Nexus. A dark presence, something ancient and powerful, that sought to corrupt the Nexus from within.

Lyra sensed it first, her eyes narrowing as she felt the malevolent energy. "There is something here, something dark and dangerous. We must findit and eradicate it before it can do any harm."

Alara and Leo joined forces with Lyra, using their combined abilities to search for the source of the darkness. It was a treacherous task, filledwith danger and uncertainty.

Their search led them to the heart of the Nexus, where they found the source of the dark presence: an ancient artifact, pulsing with a sinister energy. It was a remnant of a past battle; a weapon created to corrupt anddestroy.

"We must destroy it," Lyra said, her voice filled with determination. "If we do not, it will consume the Nexus and everything we have fought to protect."

Alara and Leo nodded, their resolve unwavering. Together, they channelled their energy into the artifact, using the power of the TemporalBeacon to counteract its malevolent influence.

The battle was fierce, the energy crackling around them like lightning. But through their combined strength and the power of their bond, they were able to destroy the artifact, its dark energy dissipating into the ether.

As the darkness lifted, a sense of peace settled over the Nexus. The groupstood together, their hearts filled with relief and triumph.

Lyra approached Alara and Leo, her eyes filled with pride. "You have proven yourselves worthy guardians of the Nexus. Your love and determination have saved us all."

Alara and Leo exchanged a glance, their hearts swelling with love and gratitude. They had faced the greatest challenges of their lives and emerged stronger for it.

That night, as they sat by the campfire, Alara and Leo took a moment to reflect on their journey. They had been through so much, but their love and determination had seen them through.

"Leo," Alara said softly, her eyes shining with tears. "I am so grateful for you. You are my strength, my hope, my everything."

Leo reached out and took her hand, his eyes filled with love. "And you are my light, Alara. Without you, I am nothing, but together, we are unstoppable—more than anyone ever imagined."

They embraced, their hearts beating as one. In that moment, they knew that no matter what challenges lay ahead, they would face them together.

With the darkness vanquished and the Nexus secure, Alara and Leo looked to the future with hope and determination. They had faced their fears and emerged stronger, their bond unbreakable.

As they stood at the entrance of the Nexus, watching the swirling energies that represented the vast expanse of time, they knew that their journey was far from over. The promise of adventure and discovery lay ahead, and they were ready to face it, side by side.

In the days that followed, they continued to train and prepare, their resolve unwavering. They knew that Veridian would return, and they needed to be ready.

But they also knew that they had the strength of their allies. and the power of their love to guide them. Together, they would face whatever came their way.

And as they looked to the horizon, they knew that the promise of adventure and discovery would always be a part of their lives, a reminder that the power of time and love could conquer any obstacle.

Chapter - 9
The Prophecy

In the days following their discovery of the Temporal Beacon, the Nexus seemed to hum with a new energy. Alara and Leo were determined to unlock its full potential, and their training sessions became more intense. They worked closely with Thalis and Lyra, pushing their limits andexploring the depths of their powers.

One afternoon, while examining an ancient text, Alara stumbled upon a passage that made her heart race. "Leo, look at this," she said, her voice filled with excitement.

Leo joined her, peering over her shoulder at the faded script. "What isit?"

"The prophecy foretells not just a battle", Alara explained. "but a war that will tear the fabric of time apart, leaving nothing but chaos in its wake that will determine the fate of the timeline. It mentions two guardians, united by love, who will face unimaginable challenges."

Leo's eyes widened. "That sounds like us."

Alara nodded. "It does. But it also mentions an ancient enemy, one who seeks to rewrite history for their own gain."

Determined to learn more about the prophecy, Alara and Leo set out on a quest to find answers. They travelled to distant realms and consulted withancient beings, uncovering fragments of knowledge that began to paint a clearer picture.

Their journey took them to the Library of Eternity, a vast repository of knowledge guarded by a wise and enigmatic librarian named Elara. She welcomed them with a knowing smile. "I have been expecting you," she said, her voice echoing through the grand halls of the library.

Alara and Leo exchanged a glance, intrigued. "You know about theprophecy?" Alara asked.

Elara nodded. "Indeed. The prophecy is ancient, and its fulfilment has been awaited for centuries. You are the chosen ones, destined to protect the timeline. But beware, for the path ahead is fraught with peril."

As they delved deeper into the prophecy, Alara and Leo were confronted with a moral dilemma. The prophecy spoke of great power, but it also warned of the dangers of using that power for personal gain.

One evening, as they sat by the campfire, Leo voiced his concerns. "What if we are not strong enough? What if we make the wrong choices?"

Alara reached out and took his hand, her eyes filled with determination. "We have come this far because of our love and our commitment to protecting the timeline. We must trust in ourselves and in each other. We will find a way."

Their conversation was interrupted by the arrival of a messenger. "A great threat approaches," he warned. "Veridian is gathering his forces. The time for the ultimate battle is near."

Realizing the gravity of the situation, Alara and Leo set out to gather allies for the impending battle. They travelled to different realms, seeking out warriors, scholars, and beings of incredible power.

Their journey led them to the Kingdom of Lumina, where they met Queen Aleria, a fierce and wise leader. She pledged her support, offering her best warriors to aid in the fight.

They also visited the Valley of Shadows, where they encountered a group of rogue fighters led by a charismatic leader named Kael. Though initially wary, Kael was won over by Alara and Leo's determination and agreed to join their cause.

As their army grew, Alara and Leo continued to study the prophecy, hoping to uncover any clues that might give them an advantage. One night, Alara had a vivid dream in which an ancient spirit revealed a crucial piece of information.

"The key to defeating Veridian lies in the heart of the Nexus," the spirit whispered. "There, you will find a hidden power, one that can turn the tide of the battle."

Alara awoke with a start, her heart pounding. She quickly relayed the dream to Leo and their allies, who agreed that they needed to find this hidden power.

With their allies at their side, Alara and Leo embarked on a perilous journey to the heart of the Nexus. The path was treacherous, filled with traps and challenges designed to assess their resolve.

As they ventured deeper into the Nexus, they encountered a series of trials that forced them to confront their deepest fears and insecurities. Butthrough it all, their love and determination carried them forward.

At last, they reached the heart of the Nexus, a place of immense power and beauty. There, they found the hidden power described in Alara's dream—a crystal of pure light, pulsating with energy.

With the crystal in their possession, Alara and Leo returned to their allies, ready to face Veridian's forces. The air was thick with tension as they prepared for the ultimate battle.

Veridian's army arrived at the Nexus, a dark and formidable force led by the Master of the Temporal Void himself. The two armies clashed with a thunderous roar, the sky filled with flashes of light and the sound of battle.

Alara and Leo fought side by side, their connection giving them the strength and courage to face even the most powerful foes. Their allies fought valiantly, each contributing their unique skills to the fight.

As the battle raged on, it became clear that Veridian's forces were formidable. The tide began to turn against Alara and her allies, and for a moment, all might be lost.

But in their darkest hour, Alara and Leo remembered the prophecy and the hidden power they had discovered. They realized that the crystal of light held the key to turning the tide of the battle.

Together, they channelled their energy into the crystal, unleashing a powerful surge of light that swept through the battlefield. The light overwhelmed Veridian's forces, disintegrating the darkness and restoring balance to the Nexus.

With his army defeated, Veridian himself stepped forward, his eyes burning with rage and desperation. "You cannot defeat me!" he roared, his voice echoing through the Nexus.

Alara and Leo stood their ground, their hearts filled with determination. "We fight for the timeline, for love, and for each other," Alara declared. "You will not prevail."

The final confrontation was fierce and intense, with Veridian unleashing his full power. But Alara and Leo, united by their love and the power of the crystal, held their ground.

In the heat of the battle, Alara and Leo realized that defeating Veridian was not just about physical strength but about understanding and compassion. They remembered the moral lesson of the prophecy—that true power lies in love and selflessness.

In a moment of clarity, Alara reached out to Verizon, offering him a chance for redemption. "It's not too late," she said.

softly. "You can choose a different path."

For a moment, Verizon hesitated, his eyes flickering with uncertainty. But then, with a final roar of defiance, he attacked with all his might.

Alara and Leo, fortified by their love and the power of the crystal, met Veridian's attack head-on. The clash of energies was blinding, filling the Nexus with a brilliant light.

When the light faded, Version was defeated, his dark power dissipating into the ether. The battlefield fell silent, the air filled with a sense of peace and triumph.

Alara and Leo stood together, their hands clasped, their hearts filled with relief and joy. They had faced unimaginable challenges and emerged victorious, their bond stronger than ever.

As the dust settled, the ancient spirit from Alara's dream appeared before them. "You have fulfilled the prophecy," the spirit said, its voice filled with pride. "Through your love and determination, you have protected the timeline and ensured a brighter future."

Alara and Leo exchanged a glance, their hearts swelling with pride and gratitude. They had faced their greatest challenge and emerged stronger for it, their love and commitment to each other unshaken.

As they looked to the future, they knew that their journey was far from over. But with their allies at their side and their bond unbreakable, they were ready to face whatever came their way.

The prophecy had been fulfilled, but the promise of adventure and discovery lay ahead. And together, Alara and Leo would continue to protect the timeline, ensuring that love and light would always prevail.

As Alara and Leo continued to study the prophecy and the power of the crystal, they discovered a hidden passage in the ancient manuscript. It spoke of a hidden realm known as the Eternal Sanctum, a place where the true source of the Nexus's power resided.

"The Eternal Sanctum," Leo mused, his eyes scanning the text. "It is said to be a place of unimaginable power, but also of great danger."

Alara nodded, her mind racing with possibilities. "If we can find it, we might be able to secure the Nexus finally. But we must be careful. The prophecy warns of great trials."

Determined to find the Eternal Sanctum, Alara and Leo gathered their allies and prepared for the journey. They knew that this quest would be they are most challenging yet, requiring all their strength and courage.

Thalis, Seraphina, Eamon, and the others pledged their support, their resolve unwavering. "We are with you, no matter what," Thalis said, his voice filled with conviction.

As they set out, Alara and Leo exchanged a glance, their hearts filled with determination. They knew that this journey would evaluate them in ways they had never imagined, but they also knew that together, they could overcome anything.

The path to the Eternal Sanctum was fraught with danger. They faced treacherous terrain, powerful guardians, and mind-bending illusions that evaluated their resolve. Each trial forced them to confront their deepest fears and insecurities.

In one particularly harrowing trial, Alara found herself facing.

A vision of her greatest fear—losing Leo. The vision was so real, so vivid, that it left her shaken to her core.

But with Leo's support, she found the strength to overcome it. "We are stronger together," he reminded her, his voice filled with love and reassurance.

After many trials, they finally reached the heart of the Eternal Sanctum. It was a place of breathtaking beauty, filled with shimmering light and anoverwhelming sense of peace.

At the centre of the Sanctum, they found the source of the Nexus's power—a crystalline structure pulsating with pure energy. As they approached, the crystal responded to their presence, its light growing brighter.

"This is it," Alara whispered, her eyes wide with wonder. "This is the source of the Nexus's power."

Leo nodded, his expression filled with awe. "We must protect it at all costs."

As they prepared to secure the crystal, they were confronted by Veridian's most powerful ally—a dark and formidable sorcerer named Malakar. His presence filled the Sanctum with a sense of dread, and his power was palpable.

"You will not succeed," Malakar snarled, his eyes blazing with fury. "The Nexus belongs to us."

Alara and Leo stood their ground, their hearts filled with determination. "We fight for the timeline, for love, and for each other," Alara declared. "You will not prevail."

The battle that ensued was fierce and intense, with Malakar unleashing his full power. But Alara and Leo, united by their love and the power of the crystal, held their ground.

During the battle, it became clear that defeating Malakar would require a great sacrifice. The crystal's energy could repel Malakar's dark power, but it required a willing heart to channel its full potential.

Alara stepped forward, her eyes filled with resolve. "I will do it," she said, her voice steady. "I will channel the crystal's power."

Leo's heart clenched with fear. "No, Alara. There must be another way."

But Alara shook her head. "This is the only way. I believe in us, Leo. Our love is stronger than anything."

With tears in his eyes, Leo nodded. "I believe in you, Alara. I will stand by your side."

As Alara channelled the crystal's energy, the light grew blindingly bright. The power surged through her, overwhelming Malakar's dark magic and restoring balance to the Sanctum.

Leo stood by her side, lending his strength and love. Together, they created a force so powerful that it shattered Malakar's defences and banished him from the Sanctum.

When the light finally faded, Alara collapsed into Leo's arms, exhausted but triumphant. "We did it," she whispered, her voice filled with relief.

Leo held her close, his heart swelling with love and gratitude. "Yes, we did. Together."

With Malakar defeated and the crystal secure, the prophecy was fulfilled. The ancient spirit from Alara's dream appeared before them once more, its voice filled with pride.

"You have proven yourselves worthy guardians of the Nexus," the spirit said. "Through your love and determination, you have protected thetimeline and ensured a brighter future."

Alara and Leo exchanged a glance, their hearts swelling with pride and gratitude. They had faced their greatest challenge and emerged stronger for it, their love and commitment to each other unshaken.

As they looked to the future, they knew that their journey was far from over. But with their allies at their side and their bond unbreakable, they were ready to face whatever came their way.

The prophecy had been fulfilled, but the promise of adventure and discovery lay ahead. And together, Alara and Leo would continue to protect the timeline, ensuring that love and light would always prevail.

As they left the Eternal Sanctum, Alara and Leo felt a renewed sense of purpose. They had faced unimaginable challenges and emerged victorious, their bond stronger than ever.

Their journey back to the Nexus was filled with moments of reflection and gratitude. They had learned so much about themselves and each other, and they were ready to face whatever came next.

Back at the Nexus, their allies welcomed them with open arms, their hearts filled with relief and joy. Thalis approached them, his eyes shining with pride. "You have done the impossible," he said. "You have secured the Nexus and ensured the future of the timeline."

With the prophecy fulfilled and the Nexus secure, Alara and Leo looked to the future with hope and determination. They knew that their journey was far from over, but they also knew that they were ready for whatever came next.

As they stood at the entrance of the Nexus, watching the swirling energies that represented the vast expanse of time, they knew that their love and determination would see them through whatever trials lay ahead.

In the days that followed, they continued to train and prepare, their resolve unwavering. They knew that Version would return, and they needed to be ready.

But they also knew that they had the strength of their allies and the power of their love to guide them. Together, they would face whatever came their way.

And as they looked to the horizon, they knew that the promise of adventure and discovery would always be a part of their lives, a reminder that the power of time and love could conquer any obstacle.

As the Nexus settled into a new era of peace, Alara and Leo took a moment to reflect on their journey. They had faced incredible challenges and emerged stronger, their bond unbreakable.

One evening, as they sat by the campfire with their allies, Alara looked at Leo, her eyes filled with love and gratitude. "We've come so far," she said softly. "And we've done it together."

Leo reached out and took her hand, his eyes shining with love. "Together, always," he replied. "No matter what comes next, we will face it together."

Their allies watched with admiration and respect, knowing that they were witnessing a bond unlike any other. Alara and Leo's love had not only saved the Nexus but had also inspired everyone around them.

As the days turned into weeks, Alara and Leo continued to protect the Nexus and the timeline. They shared their knowledge and experiences with future guardians, ensuring that the legacy of the prophecy would live on.

They built a community of guardians, each dedicated to protecting the timeline and upholding the values of love and determination. Their bond became a symbol of hope and strength, inspiring future generations to believe in the power of love and unity.

And as they looked to the future, Alara and Leo knew that their journey was far from over. They had fulfilled the prophecy, but the promise of adventure and discovery lay ahead. Together, they would continue to protect the Nexus and ensure that love and light would always prevail.

In the years that followed, Alara and Leo's bond only grew stronger. They faced new challenges and adventures, each one bringing them closer together.

Their love became a beacon of hope, guiding others through the darkest times. They knew that their journey would never truly end, but they wereready for whatever came next.

As they stood together at the entrance of the Nexus, watching the swirling energies that represented the vast expanse of time, they knew that their love would endure forever.

And as they embraced, their hearts beating as one, they knew that they had found their true purpose—to protect the timeline and ensure that loveand light would always prevail.

One night, as they rested by the campfire, Alara had a vision. She saw a future where the timeline was safe, where love and light prevailed over darkness. She saw generations of guardians, all inspired by the bond she and Leo shared.

When she awoke, she shared the vision with Leo. "I saw a future where we succeeded," she said, her voice filled with hope. "A future where our love inspired countless others to protect the timeline."

Leo smiled, his eyes shining with pride. "Then we must continue to fight for that future. We must ensure that our legacy lives on."

Just as they began to feel a sense of peace, a new threat emerged. A powerful force from a distant realm sought to corrupt the timeline, seeking to rewrite history for their own gain.

Alara and Leo knew that they could not face this new threat alone. They called upon their allies, gathering an army of guardians ready to defend the Nexus.

The new enemy was formidable, their power unlike anything Alara and Leo had faced before. But they knew that together, they could overcome any obstacle.

The battle was fierce, the enemy's power overwhelming. But Alara and Leo, fortified by their love and the support of their allies, fought with a determination that inspired everyone around them.

They used the power of the crystal and the lessons they had learned from the prophecy to counter the enemy's dark magic. Their bond gave them strength, their love a source of unyielding power.

As the battle raged on, it became clear that the enemy underestimated the power of unity and love. Alara and Leo's determination inspired their allies, and together, they began to turn the tide.

In a final climactic showdown, Alara and Leo faced the leader of the enemy forces. The dark sorcerer wielded incredible power, but Alara andLeo's bond proved to be stronger.

With the crystal's energy surging through them, they confronted the sorcerer, their love and determination guiding their every move. The sorcerer's dark magic was no match for the light and unity that Alara andLeo embodied.

In a blinding flash of light, they defeated the sorcerer, banishing the dark forces and restoring balance to the timeline.

With the enemy defeated and the timeline secure, a sense of peace settled over the Nexus. Alara and Leo stood at the centre of the Nexus, their hands clasped, their hearts filled with relief and triumph.

Their allies gathered around them, their expressions filled with admiration and respect. They had witnessed a bond unlike any other, a love that had saved the timeline and inspired countless others.

Thalis approached them, his eyes shining with pride. "You have done the impossible once again," he said. "Your love and determination havesaved us all."

As the days turned into weeks, Alara and Leo continued to protect the Nexus and the timeline. They shared their knowledge and experiences with future guardians, ensuring that the legacy of their love and determination would live on.

They built a community of guardians, each dedicated to protecting the timeline and upholding the values of love and unity. Their bond became a symbol of hope and strength, inspiring future generations to believe in the power of love.

As Alara and Leo looked to the future, they knew that their journey was far from over. They had faced unimaginable challenges and emerged stronger, their bond unbreakable.

They continued to protect the Nexus, ready to face any new threats that might arise. Their love and determination were a beacon of hope, guidingothers through the darkest times.

And as they stood together at the entrance of the Nexus, watching the swirling energies that represented the vast expanse of time, they knew that their love would endure forever.

In the years that followed, Alara and Leo's bond only grew stronger. They faced new challenges and adventures, each one bringing themcloser together.

Their love became a beacon of hope, guiding others through the darkest times. They knew that their journey would never truly end, but they wereready for whatever came next.

As they stood together at the entrance of the Nexus, watching the swirling energies that represented the vast expanse of time, they knew that their love would endure forever.

And as they embraced, their hearts beating as one, they knew that they had found their true purpose—to protect the timeline and ensure that loveand light would always prevail.

With their legacy secure and the timeline protected, Alara and Leo became known as the Eternal Guardians. Their love and determination were celebrated by all who knew them, their bond an inspiration to futuregenerations.

They continued to protect the Nexus, their hearts filled with hope and determination. They knew that the journey was far from over, but they were ready for whatever came next.

And as they stood together at the entrance of the Nexus, watching the swirling energies that represented the vast expanse of time, they knew that their love would endure forever.

Chapter - 10
The Betrayal

With the prophecy fulfilled and Version defeated, a sense of uneasy calm settled over the Nexus. Alara and Leo, though triumphant, could not shake the feeling that something was amiss.

One evening, as they sat by the campfire, Alara voiced her concerns. "Leo, I can't help but feel that this peace is temporary. There's something else out there, something we're not seeing."

Leo nodded, his brow furrowed in thought. "I feel it too. We need to stay vigilant and keep our allies close."

Their suspicions were confirmed when a mysterious stranger appeared at the Nexus. He claimed to be a messenger from a distant realm, bringing news of a new threat. His name was Draven, and his presence set everyone on edge.

Draven spoke of a hidden enemy, one that had been waiting in the shadows, planning their next move. "The battle with version was only the beginning," he warned. "The true enemy is still out there, and they are more powerful than you can imagine."

As the days passed, tensions grew within the group. Draven's presence caused division among the allies, with some questioning his motives and others eager to follow his lead.

Alara and Leo found themselves at odds with their closest allies, unsure of whom to trust. The once-united front began to crumble, and suspicionsran high.

In a shocking turn of events, it was revealed that Draven was not a messenger but a spy sent by the true enemy. His goal was to sow discord and weaken the Nexus from within.

When Alara discovered the truth, she confronted Draven, her heart heavy with betrayal. "How could you do this?" she demanded, her voice trembling with anger and hurt.

Draven smirked, his eyes cold and calculating. "You were so easy to deceive," he sneered. "The Nexus will fall, and there is nothing you can do to stop it."

As the reality of Draven's betrayal sank in, Alara and Leo knew they had to act quickly. They rallied their remaining allies, determined to root out the traitor and protect the Nexus.

In a dramatic confrontation, they exposed Draven's true intentions and banished him from the Nexus. But the damage had been done, and the group was left reeling from the betrayal.

Despite the setback, Alara and Leo refused to give up. They knew that the fight was far from over and that they needed to stay strong for the sake of the timeline.

With renewed resolve, they began to rebuild their alliances and prepare for the next battle. They knew that the road ahead would be difficult, but they were ready to face whatever challenges came their way.

The silence between Alara and Leo hung like a dark cloud. They stood in the midst of the Timekeeper's sanctuary, its once-gleaming walls now seeming cold and oppressive. The revelation that had been laid before them felt like a blow to Alara's core. Trust, fragile as it was, had been shattered by the truth.

"How could you keep this from me, Leo?" Her voice was barely more than a whisper, but it carried the weight of her heartache.

Leo turned away, unable to meet her gaze. "I didn't want to," he began, his voice strained. "I didn't know how. When I found out about my father's involvement with Veridian, I didn't know what to do. Telling you... it felt like it would break everything we've built."

Alara's hands clenched into fists, her pulse pounding in her ears. She had trusted Leo more than anyone—more than herself, even—and now, to find that he had been hiding such a critical truth from her made everything unravel.

"You should have told me," she snapped, taking a step back from him. "You should have trusted me enough to tell me. Instead, you lied by omission."

The weight of Leo's confession hung between them like a chasm, too wide to bridge. The memories of every battle they'd fought together, every sacrifice, now felt tainted by the shadow of betrayal.

Leo's eyes flashed with pain, but there was no anger in his voice. "I was afraid, Alara. Afraid of what you'd think of me if you knew the truth. My father... he's the reason Veridian gained the power to manipulate the Nexus. I couldn't bear the thought of losing you over something I didn't choose."

The betrayal stung more than any wound Alara had ever felt. But somewhere deep within her, there was also the faint echo of understanding. She knew what it was like to be bound by the mistakes of the past, to live in fear of the truth tearing everything apart.

"Leo, we can't move forward with secrets," Alara said, her voice softening, though the pain still lingered. "The Nexus thrives on truth. We can't fight Veridian if we're not fighting together."

He finally met her eyes, and for the first time, Alara saw the depths of his regret. It wasn't just guilt over what he had hidden from her—it was the fear that his choices had doomed them all.

"I'm sorry," Leo whispered, his voice barely audible.

Alara stepped closer to him, the tension between them thick enough to cut with a knife. She searched his eyes, looking for the truth she so desperately needed. Could she forgive him? Could she trust him again?

"We don't have time for apologies," she said, forcing her voice to steady. "We have to figure out our next move. Together."

For a moment, Leo remained silent, then he nodded. "Together."

The world around them felt fragile, as though the threads of time themselves were waiting for the outcome of this moment. The Nexus pulsed faintly in the distance, as if reminding them of the enormity of their task. Alara could feel its pull, a silent call to action that wouldn't allow them to linger in doubt for much longer.

Chapter - 11

The Showdown

As the allies gathered to prepare for the final showdown, the air was thick with anticipation and tension. Alara and Leo, now leaders in their own right, stood before their assembled forces, delivering a rallying speech that filled everyone with hope and determination.

Alara's voice rang out with clarity and resolve. "We have faced countless challenges, and we have overcome them all. Today, we stand together to protect the Nexus and the timeline. Together, we are unstoppable."

Leo added, "Our love and unity are our greatest strengths. We fight not just for ourselves but for the future of all realms. Let's show our enemies the power of our bond."

With their hearts filled with resolve, the allies marched toward the battlefield. The journey was long and arduous, but the bond between them grew stronger with each step. They knew that the coming battle would evaluate their limits, but they were ready to face it together.

As they approached the battlefield, they were met with the sight of Veridian's dark forces assembling. The enemy's presence was overwhelming, but Alara and Leo's determination did not waver.

The battle began with a deafening roar as the two armies clashed. The sky was filled with flashes of light and the sound of clashing weapons. Alara and Leo fought side by side, their movements synchronized and their resolve unwavering.

The allies fought valiantly, each contributing their unique skills to the fight. Thalis wielded his ancient magic, Seraphina used her agility and speed, and Eamon's strength was unmatched. Together, they formed an unbreakable force.

As the battle raged on, it became clear that Veridian's forces were formidable. The tide began to turn against the allies, and for a moment, all might be lost. But Alara and Leo refused to give up.

They rallied their allies, reminding them of the importance of their mission and the strength of their bond. With renewed determination, they fought back, their resolve unyielding.

During the chaos, Alara and Leo discovered a weakness in Veridian's forces. They realized that the enemy's power was concentrated in a sole source—a dark crystal that fuelled their strength.

With a daring plan, Alara and Leo led a group of their most trusted allies to infiltrate the enemy's ranks and destroy the crystal. The mission was dangerous, but they knew it was their only chance to turn the tide.

As they ventured deep into enemy territory, they encountered fierce resistance. But Alara and Leo's bond gave them the strength to press on. They fought their way through the enemy's defences, their determination unwavering.

At last, they reached the heart of darkness—the chamber where the dark crystal was kept. The crystal pulsed with malevolent energy, casting an eerie glow over the room.

Version himself stood before the crystal, his eyes filled with rage and determination. "You cannot defeat me," he snarled. "The Nexus belongs to me."

Alara and Leo stood their ground, their hearts filled with resolve. "We fight for the timeline, for love, and for each other," Alara declared. "You will not prevail."

The final confrontation was fierce and intense, with Version unleashing his full power. But Alara and Leo, united by their love and the power of the crystal, held their ground.

In the heat of the battle, it became clear that defeating Version would require a great sacrifice. The dark crystal's power was immense and destroying it would release a devastating surge of energy.

Alara and Leo looked at each other, their hearts heavy with the weight of their decision. "We have to do this," Leo said softly. "For the future."

Alara nodded, her eyes filled with determination. "Together."

With a final, powerful strike, they shattered the dark crystal. The resulting explosion of energy was blinding, and the force of it sent shockwaves through the battlefield.

When the light finally faded, the battlefield was silent. Version was defeated, his dark power dissipating into the ether. The allies stood in awe, their hearts filled with relief and triumph.

Alara and Leo, though exhausted, stood together, their hands clasped. They had faced unimaginable challenges and emerged victorious, their bond stronger than ever.

With the battle won and the timeline secure, Alara and Leo looked to the future with hope and determination. They knew that their journey was far from over, but they were ready for whatever came next.

As they stood at the entrance of the Nexus, watching the swirling energies that represented the vast expanse of time, they knew that their love and determination would see them through whatever trials lay ahead.

In the days that followed, they continued to train and prepare, their resolve unwavering. They knew that new challenges would come, but they were ready to face them together.

Chapter - 12
The Sacrifice

After the intense battle with Version, the Nexus experienced a brief period of peace. Alara and Leo used this time to strengthen their bonds with their allies and to prepare for any future threats.

One evening, as they sat by the campfire, Alara shared her thoughts with Leo. "We've come so far, but I can't shake the feeling that there's more to come. We need to stay vigilant."

Leo nodded, his eyes reflecting the flickering flames. "I agree. We have faced so much already, but we can't let our guard down. We'll face whatever comes together."

As they continued their preparations, an unseen threat began to stir in the shadows. A powerful entity, long forgotten and shrouded in mystery, sought to take control of the Nexus and bend time to its will.

This entity, known as the Shadow Weaver, possessed knowledge of ancient and dark magic. Its power was unlike anything Alara and Leo had faced before, and it was determined to succeed where Version had failed.

One night, Alara was visited by a vision. The ancient spirit who had guided her before appeared once more, its voice filled with urgency. "Alara, the Nexus is in grave danger. The Shadow Weaver seeks to unravel the very fabric of time. You must act quickly."

Alara awoke with a start, her heart pounding. She immediately relayed the vision to Leo and their allies, who understood the gravity of the situation.

Determined to protect the Nexus, Alara and Leo devised a plan to confront the Shadow Weaver. They knew that this battle would require not only their strength and courage but also their willingness to make the ultimate sacrifice.

"We must go to the heart of the Shadow Realm," Alara said, her voice steady. "That's where the Weaver's power is strongest. If we can confrontit there, we have a chance to stop it."

Leo took her hand, his eyes filled with resolve. "We'll face this together, no matter the cost."

With their plan in place, Alara, Leo, and their most trusted allies set out for the Shadow Realm. The journey was fraught with danger, as they traversed treacherous terrain and faced numerous challenges along the way.

Each step brought them closer to their goal, but also evaluated their resolve. The Shadow Realm was a place of darkness and despair, where the very air sapped their strength.

As they ventured deeper into the Shadow Realm, they encountered a series of trials designed to break their spirits. These trials forced them to confront their deepest fears and insecurities.

Alara faced a vision of a world where she had failed to protect the Nexus, her loved ones lost to the darkness. But with Leo's support, she found thestrength to overcome it.

Leo, too, faced his own trial, a vision of a future where he was alone and powerless. But Alara's presence reminded him of the love and unity they shared, giving him the courage to push forward.

At last, they reached the heart of the Shadow Realm, a place of unimaginable darkness. There, they confronted the Shadow Weaver, a being of pure malevolence and power.

The Weaver's eyes gleamed with a cold, calculating light. "You are brave to come here, but your efforts are futile. The Nexus will be mine."

Alara and Leo stood their ground, their hearts filled with resolve. "We fight for the timeline, for love, and for each other," Alara declared. "You will not prevail."

The ultimate battle was fierce and intense, with the Shadow Weaver unleashing its full power. Alara and Leo, united by their love and the strength of their allies, fought with everything they had.

The Weaver's dark magic clashed with the light of the Nexus, creating a storm of energy that shook the very foundations of the Shadow Realm. The battle seemed endless, each side refusing to yield.

In the heat of the battle, it became clear that defeating the Shadow Weaver would require a great sacrifice. The dark crystal's power was immense, and destroying it would release a devastating surge of energy.

Alara and Leo looked at each other, their hearts heavy with the weight of their decision. "We have to do this," Leo said softly. "For the future."

Alara nodded, her eyes filled with determination. "Together."

With a final, powerful strike, they shattered the dark crystal. The resulting explosion of energy was blinding, and the force of it sent shockwaves through the battlefield.

The ground shook violently as the dark energy erupted, and a brilliant light enveloped Alara and Leo. Their allies watched in awe and fear, uncertain of what would happen next. The energy surge was immense, threatening to consume everything in its path.

Amidst the chaos, Alara and Leo found themselves surrounded by an ethereal glow. The love they shared seemed to shield them from the destructive force, their bond creating a protective barrier. Despite the searing pain and overwhelming pressure, they held on to each other, drawing strength from their connection.

As the energy reached its peak, a deafening silence fell over the battlefield. The dark crystal shattered into countless fragments, disintegrating into nothingness. The Shadow Weaver's power, once formidable and all-encompassing, dissipated into the ether, leaving behind a profound emptiness.

When the light finally faded, the battlefield was silent. The Shadow Weaver was defeated, its dark power dissipating into the ether. The allies stood in awe, their hearts filled with relief and triumph.

Alara and Leo, though exhausted, stood together, their hands clasped. They had faced unimaginable challenges and emerged victorious, their bond stronger than ever.

With the threat of the Shadow Weaver eliminated, the Nexus was safe once more. The allies began the process of rebuilding, their hearts filled with hope for the future.

In the days that followed, the allies worked tirelessly to restore the Nexus and heal the scars left by the battle. The once-chaotic realm began to show signs of renewal, its vibrant energies slowly returning. The sense of unity among the allies grew stronger, forged through shared adversity and triumph.

As Alara and Leo walked through the rejuvenated Nexus, they could not help but reflect on their journey. They had come so far, overcome so many obstacles, and now, they stood on the precipice of a new beginning. Their bond had not only survived but thrived, becoming the cornerstone of their strength.

The ancient spirit, who had guided Alara throughout her journey, appeared once more. "You have done well, Alara and Leo. The Nexus is safe, and the timeline is secure. Your love and determination have prevailed."

Alara bowed her head in gratitude. "Thank you for your guidance. We couldn't have done it without you."

The spirit smiled, a warm light emanating from its form. "Your journey is far from over. The future holds many challenges, but I have no doubt that you will face them with the same courage and resolve."

Leo squeezed Alara's hand. "We'll be ready. Together."

Chapter - 13
The Turning Point

After defeating the Shadow Weaver, Alara and Leo faced a new challenge. The Nexus, though secure, required constant vigilance and protection.

Despite the victory, they knew that new threats could emerge at any time. The responsibility of guarding the Nexus weighed heavily on their shoulders, but they were determined to protect it at all costs.

One day, while exploring the Nexus, they discovered a hidden chamber filled with ancient knowledge. This discovery provided new insights into the Nexus and its powers, offering hope for a brighter future.

The chamber contained ancient texts and artifacts, each holding secrets about the Nexus's true potential. As they delved deeper into the knowledge, they realized that the Nexus had the ability to heal and rejuvenate not just itself but the surrounding realms.

With this newfound knowledge, Alara and Leo felt a renewed sense of purpose. They vowed to protect the Nexus and ensure that its secrets would be used for the greater good.

They began to share their findings with their allies, fostering a sense of unity and shared responsibility. Together, they worked to unlock the full potential of the Nexus, creating a haven of peace and prosperity.

Alara couldn't shake the feeling that something was wrong. The landscape around her, once so familiar, now felt like an alien world. The Nexus had been their guide, their compass, but now it seemed to be leading them into uncharted territory—both in the physical sense and in her heart.

"Do you feel it too?" Leo asked, his voice soft but edged with tension.

Alara nodded, her emerald eyes scanning the horizon. "The Nexus is... different. It's like something has shifted, and I can't figure out why."

The air around them crackled with energy, the faint hum of the Nexus growing louder with each passing moment. Alara could feel its power vibrating through her, a constant reminder that they were walking on the edge of a precipice.

"We need to figure out what's changed," Leo said, his brow furrowed in thought. "This might be the turning point we've been waiting for, but it could also be the moment everything falls apart."

Alara's heart raced as she considered his words. The Nexus had always been unpredictable, but now it felt as though it was actively working against them. Every step they took felt like a gamble, and the stakes couldn't have been higher.

The ground beneath them shifted, and suddenly, they were surrounded by a swirling vortex of light and shadow. Alara's breath caught in her throat as the threads of time twisted and bent around them, pulling them in every direction at once. It was disorienting, and for a moment, she feared they would be torn apart by the force of it.

But then, just as quickly as it began, the vortex stilled, and they found themselves standing in the heart of the Nexus. The crystalline structure loomed before them, its spires shimmering with an otherworldly light. Alara felt a sense of awe wash over her as she gazed at it, but beneath that awe was a growing sense of dread.

"This is it," Leo said, his voice barely above a whisper. "This is where everything changes."

Alara stepped forward, her hand outstretched toward the Nexus. She could feel its power pulsing beneath her fingertips, a steady rhythm that echoed in her bones. The Nexus was alive, and it was waiting for her to make the next move.

But what that move was, Alara didn't know. All she knew was that the path ahead was uncertain, and the decisions they made now would determine the fate of everything.

Chapter – 14
Aftermath

In the wake of the ultimate battle, the allies worked tirelessly to rebuild the Nexus and heal the wounds of the past. Alara and Leo led the efforts, their bond stronger than ever.

The Nexus began to flourish once more, its energies vibrant and life- giving. The allies dedicated themselves to creating a safe and harmonious environment, ensuring that the sacrifices made were not in vain.

As they rebuilt, they took time to reflect on their journey. They remembered the challenges they had faced, the sacrifices they had made, and the love that had carried them through.

Alara and Leo often found themselves reminiscing about their adventures, each memory a testament to their resilience and growth. They had faced darkness and emerged stronger, their bond unbreakable.

They honoured the memory of those who had fallen in battle, ensuring that their sacrifices would never be forgotten. Memorials were erected, and stories were shared, preserving the legacy of their bravery.

Ceremonies were held to pay tribute to the fallen, their names etched in the annals of history. The allies vowed to protect the Nexus in their honour, carrying forward the torch of their courage.

With the Nexus restored, they looked to the future with hope and determination. They knew that new challenges would come, but they were ready to face them together.

The realms began to thrive once more, the Nexus's influence reaching everywhere. Prosperity and peace became the new norm, a stark contrast to the chaos that had once threatened to consume them.

Alara and Leo worked to strengthen their alliances, ensuring that the Nexus would be protected by a united front. They knew that unity was their greatest strength.

Diplomatic efforts were made to forge stronger ties with neighbouring realms, creating a network of support and collaboration. Together, they established a council dedicated.to safeguarding the Nexus and its secrets.

As they looked to the future, they embraced the lessons they had learned and the strength they had gained. They knew that their love and determination would see them through whatever trials lay ahead.

Alara and Leo continued to train and prepare, honing their skills and deepening their bond. They were ready to face any challenge that came their way, their hearts filled with unwavering resolve.

With the Nexus secure, they ushered in a new era of peace and prosperity. They knew that their journey was far from over, but they were ready for whatever came next.

The realms flourished under their guardianship, each day a testament to their dedication and love. The Nexus became a beacon of hope, a symbol of the enduring power of unity and resilience.

Their story became a legend, a testament to the power of love and the strength of the human spirit. They knew that their legacy would live on, inspiring future generations to protect the Nexus and cherish the bonds of love and unity.

The tales of Alara and Leo's journey were passed down through the ages, their love story becoming an inspiration to all. They had faced insurmountable odds and emerged victorious, their legacy a shining example of what could be achieved through love and determination.

Chapter - 15
New Beginnings

With the Nexus secure and their enemies defeated, Alara and Leo embraced a new beginning. They looked forward to the future with hope and determination.

The sense of peace and fulfilment that came with their victory allowed them to explore new opportunities and dreams. They were excited to embark on this new chapter of their lives together.

They began to build a life together, cherishing the love and unity that had carried them through their journey. They knew that their bond was unbreakable.

Their days were filled with joy and laughter, their love growing stronger with each passing moment. They found comfort in the simple pleasures of life, knowing that they had overcome so much to be where they were.

As they looked to the future, they knew that they would face new challenges and adventures. But they were ready, their hearts filled with hope and determination.

Together, they continued to explore the Nexus and its secrets, eager to unlock its full potential. They knew that their journey was far from over, but they were excited to face whatever lay ahead.

The air was thick with the scent of rain, the first drops falling softly on the leaves as Alara and Leo walked through the forest. The world around them was quiet, save for the distant rumble of thunder on the horizon. It was a moment of peace, but Alara knew it wouldn't last.

"Do you think we did the right thing?" Leo asked, his voice barely above a whisper.

Alara looked at him, her heart heavy with the weight of their decisions. "I don't know," she admitted. "But I do know that we did what we had to do."

Leo nodded, though the uncertainty in his eyes remained. They had faced so much, lost so much, and now they were left with the aftermath. The Nexus was gone, the threads of time severed, and the world they had fought so hard to protect was now theirs to rebuild.

"It feels strange, doesn't it?" Alara continued. "To have fought so hard for something, only to realize that the real battle is just beginning."

Leo smiled faintly, though it didn't quite reach his eyes. "New beginnings," he said softly. "That's what you called it, right? I guess we're about to find out what that really means."

They continued walking, the silence between them comfortable yet filled with unspoken thoughts. Alara could feel the weight of the past pressing down on her, but she also felt a glimmer of hope for the future. They had survived, and now they had the chance to rebuild, to create something new out of the ashes of what was lost.

For the first time in a long time, Alara allowed herself to believe that maybe, just maybe, everything would be okay.

Chapter – 16

Reflections

As they settled into their new life, Alara and Leo took time to reflect on their journey. They remembered the challenges they had faced, the sacrifices they had made, and the love that had carried them through.

Their reflections brought a sense of gratitude and pride, knowing that they had accomplished so much together. They had faced darkness and emerged stronger, their bond unbreakable.

They embraced the lessons they had learned and the strength they had gained. They knew that their experiences had made them stronger and more resilient.

They used these lessons to guide their actions, ensuring that they continued to grow and evolve. They were committed to becoming better guardians and better people, using their past experiences as a foundation for their future.

Their story became a legend, a testament to the power of love and the strength of the human spirit. They knew that their legacy would live on, inspiring future generations to protect the Nexus and cherish the bonds of love and unity.

They were often approached by young guardians seeking guidance and inspiration. Alara and Leo took these opportunities to share their story, hoping to instil the same sense of hope and determination in others.

As they looked to the future, they embraced the lessons they had learned and the strength they had gained. They knew that their love and determination would see them through whatever trials lay ahead.

They continued to dream and plan, setting new goals and aspirations. They knew that their journey was far from over, but they were excited to face whatever lay ahead.

They remained dedicated to protecting the Nexus and ensuring its continued prosperity. Their love and unity were their greatest strengths, and they were ready to face any challenge that came their way.

The weight of the battle clung to the air, a tangible reminder of the struggle that had brought them to this moment. Alara stood at the edge of the cliff, her emerald-green eyes gazing out at the vast horizon. The sky, once turbulent and dark, was now painted with hues of gold and soft lavender as the sun began to set. It was the first time in days that she had felt anything resembling peace, but peace was elusive—a fleeting illusion in a world still reeling from the effects of the Nexus.

Alara's mind wandered back to the events that had led them here. The battles fought, the lives lost, and the sacrifices made all seemed to blur together in her memory. Yet, there were moments that stood out, etched in her mind like scars she would never forget. She could still feel the pulse of the Nexus beneath her fingertips, the overwhelming power that had threatened to consume everything.

But now, the Nexus was gone, and the world had to continue without its guiding force. The future stretched out before them, uncertain and daunting.

Leo approached her from behind, his footsteps quiet but sure. He stopped beside her, his gaze also fixed on the horizon. For a moment, neither of them spoke, the silence between them filled with the unspoken understanding that had always defined their bond.

"Do you think we'll ever stop feeling it?" Alara asked softly, her voice barely more than a whisper.

Leo tilted his head slightly, considering her question. "Feeling what?"

"The pull of the Nexus. The weight of everything that happened."

Leo's piercing blue eyes softened as he looked at her, his expression both comforting and conflicted. "I don't know. But I think it will always be with us, in some way. We're connected to it, even now. It's a part of us."

Alara let out a slow breath, nodding. "I just... I thought when this was over, I would feel free. Like we'd won, and everything would go back to the way it was. But nothing feels like it used to."

Leo reached out, gently placing a hand on her shoulder. "Things can never go back to the way they were. But maybe that's not such a bad thing. We have a chance now—a chance to shape the future in a way we couldn't before. Without the Nexus controlling everything, we can decide our own path."

Alara glanced at him, her heart heavy with the burden of responsibility. "But what if we make the wrong choices? What if we fail?"

Leo's hand tightened slightly on her shoulder, his voice firm yet reassuring. "We won't. We've come this far, Alara. We've faced the impossible and survived. Whatever comes next, we'll face it together. And we'll figure it out."

The words brought a small, tentative smile to Alara's lips. It wasn't much, but it was enough to remind her that she wasn't alone. They had been through too much to falter now, and though the road ahead was uncertain, they had each other.

As the sun dipped lower on the horizon, casting long shadows across the landscape, Alara turned her thoughts inward. She couldn't shake the feeling that something was still unresolved, something lurking beneath the surface of everything they had fought for. The Nexus was gone, but its influence lingered, like an echo reverberating through time.

"There's still so much we don't understand," she said quietly, more to herself than to Leo.

Leo nodded, his expression thoughtful. "That's true. The Nexus may be destroyed, but its impact on time, on the world... we're only beginning to see the effects."

Alara's mind raced with the possibilities. What had they truly unleashed by destroying the Nexus? The threads of time were no longer bound to the Nexus's control, and while that had seemed like a victory, it also meant that time itself was now in a state of flux. They had won the battle, but the war with time was far from over.

"We need to keep looking for answers," she said, her voice gaining strength. "We need to understand what the Nexus really was, and what happens now that it's gone."

Leo smiled softly, a hint of admiration in his eyes. "Always the curious one, aren't you?"

Alara chuckled, though the sound was laced with exhaustion. "I guess some things never change."

For a while longer, they stood in silence, watching as the last rays of sunlight disappeared beneath the horizon. The night crept in, bringing with it a cool breeze that sent a shiver down Alara's spine. But it wasn't the cold that unsettled her—it was the unknown. The uncertainty of what lay ahead.

Finally, Leo spoke again, his voice low and steady. "What do you think happens next?"

Alara turned her gaze toward him, her thoughts still swirling. "I don't know. But whatever it is, we have to be ready. The world is different now, and we're going to have to adapt."

Leo nodded in agreement. "We will. Together."

The words brought a sense of comfort, but Alara knew it was only temporary. The road ahead was long, and there were still too many unanswered questions. But for now, in this moment, she allowed herself to believe that they would find a way forward. They had to.

As the stars began to appear in the darkening sky, Alara felt a renewed sense of purpose. The battle might have been over, but their journey was far from complete. There was still so much to learn, so much to understand about the Nexus, time, and their place within it.

"We'll find the answers," Alara said with quiet determination. "No matter how long it takes."

Leo's smile widened, his eyes filled with a sense of hope. "I believe you."

With that, they turned away from the cliff and began walking back toward the others. The future awaited them, filled with uncertainty and promise in equal measure. And though the Nexus was gone, its legacy would remain with them—forever intertwined with their fates.

Together, they would face whatever came next. And no matter what challenges awaited them, Alara knew one thing for certain: They would face it as one.

Chapter – 17
The Legacy

With the Nexus secure and their enemies defeated, Alara and Leo began a new chapter in their lives. They looked forward to the future with hope and determination.

They continued to explore the realms, discovering unfamiliar places and cultures. Each adventure brought them closer, their love deepening as they shared these experiences. They learned to appreciate the beauty in the world around them, finding peace in their shared journey.

They began to build a life together, cherishing the love and unity that had carried them through their journey. They knew that their bond was unbreakable.

Their days were filled with joy and laughter, their love growing stronger with each passing moment. They found comfort in the simple pleasures of life, knowing that they had overcome so much to be where they were.

As they settled into their new life, Alara and Leo embraced the changes that came with it. They welcomed new challenges and opportunities, knowing that they could face anything together.

They took on new roles within the Nexus, using their skills and knowledge to help others. Alara became a mentor to young guardians, sharing her wisdom and experience. Leo took on the role of a strategist, using his keen mind to plan.

As they looked to the future, they knew that they would face new challenges and adventures. But they were ready, their hearts filled with hope and determination.

They continued to dream and plan, setting new goals and aspirations. They knew that their journey was far from over, but they were excited to face whatever lay ahead.

Alara and Leo stood in the heart of the Chrono Nexus, the swirling energies reflecting in their wide eyes. As they approached the central pedestal, a sense of awe and trepidation washed over them. The pedestal held a crystal orb, pulsating with a soft, ethereal light. This was the Heart of Time, the artifact that controlled the very fabric of existence.

Leo reached out tentatively, his hand hovering above the orb. "This is it, Alara. This is what we've been searching for."

Alara nodded, her heart pounding. "We have to be careful, Leo. One wrong move and we could alter everything."

Just as Leo was about to touch the orb, a voice echoed through the chamber. "Stop!"

They turned to see Seraphina, the ancient guardian they had encountered before, emerging from the shadows. Her expression was a mix of determination and fear. "You do not understand the power you are dealing with. The Heart of Time is not just a tool; it is a living entity."

Alara frowned. "What do you mean?"

Seraphina stepped closer, her eyes locking onto the orb. "The Heart of Time has a consciousness. It can sense your intentions and act accordingly. If you are not pure of heart, it will reject you and unleash chaos."

Leo withdrew his hand, looking at Alara. "We have to prove ourselves worthy."

Seraphina nodded. "To do that, you must face the Trials of Time. Only then will the Heart accept you."

The Trials of Time were legendary, spoken of in hushed tones among the guardians. Alara and Leo had no choice but to face them if they were to fulfill their destiny.

The first trial was the Trial of Reflection. Alara and Leo found themselves in a hall of mirrors, each reflecting different moments of their past. They had to confront their deepest fears and regrets. Alara saw herself struggling with the loss of her parents, while Leo faced his guilt over past mistakes. Through tears and determination, they accepted their past, vowing to learn and grow from it.

Next was the Trial of Sacrifice. They were transported to a desolate landscape, where a loved one stood at the edge of a cliff, teetering on the brink of falling. For Alara, it was her grandfather, and for Leo, it was his younger sister. They had to choose between saving their loved ones and completing the trial. With heavy hearts, they made the ultimate sacrifice, understanding that their mission was greater than personal desires.

The final trial was the Trial of Unity. Alara and Leo found themselves separated in a labyrinth, facing various challenges that required trust and cooperation. They had to communicate through their bond, relying on each other's strengths to navigate the maze. Despite the physical separation, their connection grew stronger, proving their unity and commitment to their cause.

Having successfully completed the Trials of Time, Alara and Leo stood once again before the Heart of Time. Seraphina watched silently as they approached the pedestal, their faces reflecting determination and newfound wisdom.

Alara placed her hand on the orb, feeling a surge of energy flow through her. The Heart of Time glowed brighter, its light enveloping her. "We come with pure intentions," she whispered. "We seek to restore balance and protect the timeline."

Leo joined her, his hand covering hers on the orb. "Together, we are stronger. We vow to uphold the legacy of the guardians and ensure that time remains unbroken."

The Heart of Time pulsed with approval, its light intensifying. A voice, ancient and powerful, resonated within their minds. "You have proven yourselves worthy. The power of time is yours to wield, but remember, with great power comes great responsibility."

As the light subsided, Alara and Leo felt a profound connection to the Heart of Time. They understood the weight of their mission and the sacrifices required. Seraphina approached them, her expression softening. "You have done well. The legacy of the guardians lives on through you."

Alara and Leo shared a determined look. "We won't let you down," Alarapromised.

With the Heart of Time now in their possession, they knew their journey was far from over. The path ahead was fraught with challenges, but they were ready. Together, they would face whatever came their way, armed with the power of time and their unwavering bond.

Chapter - 18
The Quantum Bond

The Nexus seemed to pulse around them, each ripple through time more pronounced than the last. Alara could feel it in her bones, in her soul—this connection that she had to Leo was something far beyond anything she had experienced before. Every breath she took felt synchronized with his, every thought seemed to echo between them. It was as if they were two pieces of the same whole, drawn together by forces far greater than either of them.

"Alara, do you think this was always meant to be?" Leo asked, his voice quiet but filled with wonder.

She glanced at him, seeing the confusion and awe in his eyes. "Meant to be... I don't know," she replied, her voice trembling slightly. "But it's undeniable now. We're connected in ways that go beyond anything I can explain. It's not just our fates... it's our very existence."

The realization weighed heavily on both of them. Quantum entanglement was a concept Alara had learned about in her studies—a strange phenomenon in which particles, once connected, remained linked no matter the distance between them. What affected one affected the other instantly, across any space and time. But this was different. This was human.

"It feels like more than just a connection," Leo said, running his fingers through his hair as he tried to make sense of it all. "It feels like... I don't even know how to describe it. Like every fiber of my being is intertwined with yours."

Alara reached out, taking his hand in hers. "I know," she whispered. "I feel it too. But what does it mean for us? For everything?"

As they continued deeper into the Nexus, the swirling energy around them intensified. The colors became more vivid, shifting in and out of focus as if the very fabric of reality was bending to their presence. Time was no longer linear here—it twisted and looped around them, like threads in an intricate web that had no beginning or end.

At that moment, Alara could feel Leo's fear as clearly as her own. It wasn't just empathy—it was as though his emotions were flowing through her, becoming her own.

"Leo," she said softly, "I'm scared too. But we have to keep going. We have to understand what this is."

Leo nodded, his grip on her hand tightening. "I know. But what if we can't control it? What if this bond becomes... something we can't break?"

A chill ran down Alara's spine. The thought had crossed her mind more than once—that their connection wasn't just a blessing, but also a curse. If they were truly quantum entangled, then their lives were now bound together in ways they couldn't begin to comprehend. If one of them were hurt... if one of them were to die...

She couldn't even bring herself to finish the thought.

"We have to figure it out," she said firmly, pushing her fears aside. "We have to find a way to control it, to understand it. Before it's too late."

The Nexus shifted again, and they found themselves standing in what appeared to be a vast hall, its walls shimmering with the energy of countless timelines. The air was thick with the hum of the Nexus's power, and in the center of the room stood a large, crystalline structure—the heart of the Nexus.

"This is it," Alara said, her voice filled with awe. "This is the source of the Nexus's power."

Leo stared at the crystalline structure, his eyes wide. "It's beautiful... and terrifying."

As they approached the structure, Alara felt the pull of the Nexus growing stronger. It wasn't just pulling at her body—it was pulling at her very soul, at the bond she shared with Leo. The closer they got, the more intense the connection became, until it felt as though they were no longer two separate beings, but one.

"We can't stay here for long," Alara said, her voice strained. "The Nexus is amplifying the bond. If we stay too long... we might lose ourselves in it."

Leo nodded, though she could see the hesitation in his eyes. "But what if this is the only way to understand it? What if the answers we're looking for are here?"

Alara hesitated, torn between the desire to understand the bond and the fear of what it might cost them. "We have to be careful, Leo. We're walking a fine line here. One wrong move, and we might not be able to come back."

As they stood before the crystalline structure, something strange began to happen. The Nexus's energy seemed to coalesce around them, wrapping them in a cocoon of light. Alara could feel the bond between them growing stronger, more tangible, as though the very essence of the Nexus was fusing them together.

"Leo... do you feel that?" she asked, her voice trembling.

"I do," he replied, his eyes wide with wonder. "It's like... the Nexus is trying to show us something."

Suddenly, images began to flash before their eyes—visions of the past, the present, and the future, all blending together in a dizzying array of light and color. They saw themselves as children, unaware of the destiny that awaited them. They saw their journey through the Nexus, the trials they had faced, and the battles yet to come. And they saw the future—a future where their bond had become something far greater than either of them could have imagined.

But there was something else too. Something darker.

In the depths of the visions, Alara caught a glimpse of Veridian. His eyes burned with fury, his hands reaching out as though to tear them apart. She could feel his hatred, his desire to destroy them, to break the bond that tied them together.

"Veridian..." she whispered, her voice filled with fear.

Leo's hand tightened around hers. "We have to stop him, Alara. We can't let him destroy everything we've fought for."

Alara nodded, her resolve hardening. "We will. But first... we have to survive this."

As the visions faded, they found themselves standing once more in the heart of the Nexus, the crystalline structure glowing softly before them. The bond between them was stronger than ever, but it was also more fragile. They were quantum entangled, connected in ways that defied understanding. But with that connection came a risk—a risk that could destroy them both.

"We have to be careful," Alara said, her voice firm. "If something happens to one of us…"

Leo nodded, his expression grim. "I know. But we'll face it together."

They stood there in silence for a moment, the weight of their bond heavy on their shoulders. But despite the fear, despite the uncertainty, they knew one thing for certain: they would fight for each other, no matter the cost.

The Nexus hummed louder now, the energy swirling around them growing more erratic with each passing second. Alara's chest tightened as she felt the weight of her quantum connection to Leo bearing down on her. Every beat of her heart seemed to sync with his, their breaths aligned as if they were part of the same organism.

"We need to understand why the Nexus has tied us like this," Alara said, her voice barely above a whisper. "This isn't just about us—there's something much bigger happening here."

Leo nodded, his eyes fixed on the crystal at the center of the Nexus. "The Nexus doesn't do anything by accident," he muttered, his brow furrowed in concentration. "It's using us. Somehow, we're the key to everything."

Alara's breath was shallow, each inhale more difficult than the last as the pressure of the Nexus wrapped around them like a vice. The crystalline structure in the center glowed brighter, casting sharp shadows that danced across the walls of the void. She could feel the pulse of the Nexus within her, resonating with the connection she shared with Leo. It wasn't just pulling them closer—it was merging them into one.

"We have to figure this out, Leo," Alara said, her voice strained. "The Nexus is doing something to us, something we're not ready for."

Leo's gaze was fixed on the glowing structure ahead. His expression was a mix of awe and determination. "I know," he replied. "But I can feel it too—there's something here, something we need to understand. If we walk away now, we might lose the only chance we have to unravel this bond."

Alara could feel his fear, his uncertainty, but also his unwavering resolve. It was the same feeling she had, mirrored perfectly in his thoughts. Their bond wasn't just emotional—it was quantum, an unbreakable link that tied them together in ways that transcended time and space.

The ground beneath them began to tremble, and the air around them crackled with energy. Alara glanced at the crystal, watching as the swirling light inside it intensified, becoming more chaotic with every passing second.

"We're running out of time," she whispered, her heart pounding in her chest. "The Nexus is destabilizing."

Leo took a step forward, his eyes locked on the crystal. "We have to stabilize it. Whatever's happening here, it's tied to us. The bond, the Nexus, everything—it's all connected."

Alara followed him, her steps tentative but purposeful. As they approached the crystal, the energy around them surged, the air growing heavy with the weight of countless timelines converging in one place. She could feel the pull of the future, the past, and every possible version of herself that could exist.

"Alara," Leo said softly, turning to face her. "I don't know what's going to happen, but I trust you. I trust us. Whatever this bond is, it's part of something bigger than either of us. We can't be afraid of it."

She looked into his eyes and saw the depth of their connection reflected back at her. It wasn't just love—it was a force that defied the very laws of the universe. Quantum entanglement was a scientific concept, but what they were experiencing went beyond that. It was as though the Nexus had chosen them, binding them together in ways that no one could ever hope to explain.

Alara took a deep breath and reached out toward the crystal. Her fingers hovered just above its surface, and she could feel the raw power radiating from it. The moment she touched it, the world around them exploded in a burst of light and sound. The ground shook violently, and Alara was thrown backward, her connection to Leo flickering like a dying flame.

"Alara!" Leo shouted, his voice barely audible over the roaring energy that now filled the air.

She scrambled to her feet, her heart racing as she searched for him in the chaos. The Nexus was coming apart, the timelines unraveling before her eyes. Every second felt like an eternity, each moment stretched to its breaking point.

"I'm here!" Alara shouted, her voice hoarse as she fought against the swirling wind and light. "I'm right here!"

But just as she reached for him, something strange happened. The bond between them snapped into focus, clearer than it had ever been before. She could feel his heartbeat, his thoughts, his very essence—everything that made Leo who he was. And then, in a sudden moment of clarity, she understood.

The Nexus hadn't just connected them. It had fused them. They weren't just two people linked by fate; they were one entity, bound together in ways that defied explanation.

"We're not just connected," Alara whispered, her voice trembling with realization. "We're the same. The Nexus... it's made us one."

Leo's eyes widened as he felt it too. "But how? How is that even possible?"

"It's the Nexus," she replied, her voice filled with awe. "It's more than just a conduit for time. It's alive, Leo. It's sentient. And it's chosen us."

Page 226:

The Nexus pulsed again, the light within it flickering like a heartbeat. Alara could feel the surge of energy coursing through her, but it was no longer overwhelming. It was familiar, almost comforting. The bond between her and Leo had been solidified, cemented by the Nexus itself.

But with that bond came new responsibilities—new dangers.

"The Nexus has given us power," Alara said, her voice steady despite the chaos around them. "But it's also made us vulnerable. If we're one, then if something happens to one of us..."

She couldn't bring herself to finish the thought, but Leo understood. He nodded grimly, his expression serious. "Then we both fall," he said softly. "We're stronger together, but that means we're also at greater risk."

Alara's mind raced as she tried to process the implications of their newfound connection. The bond was a gift, but it was also a curse. They had gained a power that few could even comprehend, but it came with a price.

"We have to find a way to control it," Leo said, his voice filled with determination. "We can't let this bond control us."

Alara nodded, her resolve hardening. "We will. But first... we need to figure out why the Nexus did this to us. There has to be a reason."

They turned their attention back to the crystal, which still pulsed with the same strange energy as before. It was the key to everything—the source of the Nexus's power and the answer to their questions.

But as they approached it again, the air around them shifted. Alara felt a cold chill run down her spine, and her heart skipped a beat. Something wasn't right.

"Do you feel that?" she asked, her voice barely above a whisper.

Leo nodded, his eyes scanning the void around them. "Yeah. We're not alone."

Page 230:

Suddenly, a figure emerged from the shadows, its presence sending a wave of dread through Alara's chest. It was Veridian.

His eyes glowed with a malevolent light, and the air around him seemed to distort as if time itself was bending to his will. Alara's heart raced as she took a step back, her body tense with fear.

"You've done well," Veridian said, his voice smooth and cold. "But your journey ends here. The Nexus belongs to me. And so do you."

Alara's breath caught in her throat as Veridian raised his hand, summoning the energy of the Nexus. The air crackled with power, and the ground trembled beneath their feet.

"We can't let him take the Nexus," Leo whispered, his voice filled with urgency. "We have to stop him."

Alara nodded, her fear quickly turning to determination. "We will. Together."

Page 235:

The battle that followed was unlike anything they had ever experienced. Veridian's power was immense, fueled by the Nexus itself. But Alara and Leo had something he didn't—each other.

The bond between them pulsed with energy, amplifying their strength and abilities. Every move they made was perfectly synchronized, as if they were two parts of the same whole. They fought as one, their connection giving them the edge they needed to hold their ground against Veridian's onslaught.

But as the battle raged on, Alara realized something else—something far more terrifying. The bond between her and Leo wasn't just making them stronger. It was draining them. Every time they tapped into the Nexus's power, it took something from them in return. They were burning through their energy, their very life force, faster than they could sustain.

"We're running out of time," Alara gasped, her voice filled with panic. "We can't keep this up."

Leo's face was pale, his body trembling from the strain. "We have to finish this. Now."

Alara's breath came in ragged gasps as she and Leo faced Veridian, the swirling energies of the Nexus crackling around them like a living storm. Every strike they made against him sent ripples through the very fabric of time, but Veridian was relentless, feeding off the power of the Nexus as though it had always been his to command.

The connection between Alara and Leo surged with every movement, their bond amplifying their abilities to a level they had never imagined. But with each surge of power, Alara could feel a piece of herself slipping away, as if the Nexus was draining her very essence in exchange for the strength it gave her.

"We're using too much of the Nexus's power," Alara whispered, her voice strained. "It's pulling us in... taking more than we can give."

Leo nodded, his face pale with exertion. "I know. But we have to finish this. We can't let Veridian control the Nexus. If he gets it..."

The thought was too terrifying to finish. Veridian with control over time itself would mean the end of everything they knew. The balance of the universe would shift, and the consequences would be catastrophic.

Veridian's eyes gleamed with malice as he raised his hands, summoning a torrent of energy from the Nexus. The ground beneath them trembled violently, and the air became thick with the hum of power. Alara could feel the pressure building, a force so immense that it threatened to tear them apart.

"You've only just begun to understand what the Nexus is capable of," Veridian said, his voice echoing with the power of a thousand timelines. "But you'll never be able to control it. You're weak. You're nothing."

Alara's heart raced, her body trembling from the strain of holding the bond together. She could feel Leo beside her, his presence a constant source of strength, but it wasn't enough. They were running out of time.

"We're not nothing," Leo said, his voice strong despite the exhaustion that weighed on him. "We're connected. We're stronger together than you could ever understand."

With a final burst of energy, Leo lunged toward Veridian, his movements fueled by the bond that tied him to Alara. Time seemed to slow as he reached out, his hand glowing with the energy of the Nexus, but Veridian was faster. He deflected Leo's attack with a wave of his hand, sending him crashing to the ground with a sickening thud.

"Leo!" Alara screamed, her heart lurching as she felt the impact reverberate through their bond. She could feel his pain as if it were her own, the searing agony spreading through her chest like wildfire.

Veridian's laughter filled the air, cold and cruel. "You should have known better than to challenge me. The Nexus is mine, and now… so are you."

Alara's vision blurred, her body trembling from the strain of the bond. Every instinct screamed at her to run, to escape before the Nexus consumed her entirely, but she couldn't leave Leo behind. She wouldn't.

Drawing on the last reserves of her strength, Alara pushed herself to her feet, her eyes locking onto Veridian's. She could feel the Nexus pulsing within her, the power of time itself coursing through her veins. It was overwhelming, suffocating, but she couldn't afford to hold back any longer.

"This ends now," she said, her voice steady despite the fear that gripped her heart.

Veridian sneered, his eyes narrowing as he raised his hand to strike her down, but before he could, Alara unleashed the full force of the Nexus. The energy erupted from her in a blinding wave of light, tearing through the air with a deafening roar. Time itself seemed to shatter, fragments of past and future swirling around them in a chaotic maelstrom.

For a moment, everything stopped. The world was silent, frozen in the wake of the power that had been unleashed.

And then, as quickly as it had begun, the storm dissipated. The air was still, the energy of the Nexus settling into a gentle hum.

Veridian was gone—his form dissipated into nothingness, consumed by the very power he had sought to control.

Alara collapsed to the ground, her body trembling from the effort of wielding the Nexus's power. She could feel the bond between her and Leo still pulsing faintly, but it was weaker now, more fragile than ever.

"Leo…" she whispered, her voice barely audible. She crawled toward him, her heart pounding in her chest as she reached his side.

He lay motionless on the ground, his face pale and his breathing shallow. Alara's chest tightened with fear as she placed her hand on his shoulder, her fingers trembling.

"Please," she whispered, her voice cracking with emotion. "Please don't leave me."

For a moment, there was only silence. The world seemed to hang in limbo, suspended between hope and despair. And then, slowly, Leo's eyes fluttered open.

"Alara..." he whispered, his voice weak but steady. "We... we did it."

Tears filled her eyes as she pulled him into her arms, her heart swelling with relief. "I thought I lost you," she whispered, her voice trembling with emotion.

Leo smiled weakly, his hand reaching up to cup her cheek. "You'll never lose me," he said softly. "Not as long as we're connected."

Alara rested her forehead against his, her tears falling freely as the weight of everything they had been through washed over her. The battle was over, but the bond between them remained—fragile, yet unbreakable.

They had survived, but the cost had been high. The Nexus had changed them, fused them together in ways they could never have imagined. Their connection was stronger than ever, but it was also more dangerous. If one of them fell, the other would follow.

But for now, in this moment, they were alive. And that was enough.

The energy of the Nexus continued to pulse softly around them, its presence a constant reminder of the power they had wielded and the price they had paid. Alara could feel the weight of the bond pressing down on her, but she no longer feared it. The connection she shared with Leo was not something to be feared—it was something to be cherished.

As she held him close, she whispered softly, "We're going to figure this out, Leo. We'll learn to control it... together."

Leo nodded, his eyes closing as he rested his head against her shoulder. "Together," he repeated, his voice barely above a whisper.

For a long time, they sat there in the stillness of the Nexus, their hearts beating in perfect harmony. The storm had passed, and for the first time in what felt like an eternity, the future seemed... possible.

But even as they rested, Alara couldn't shake the feeling that their journey was far from over. The Nexus had given them a gift, but it had also set them on a path that neither of them could fully understand. There were still mysteries to uncover, still dangers lurking in the shadows.

And somewhere, in the farthest reaches of time, Alara could sense it—a darkness, growing ever closer.

She closed her eyes, her hand tightening around Leo's. Whatever lay ahead, they would face it together. And no matter what the future held, their bond would carry them through.

As the minutes passed, the reality of what had just happened settled over them like a dense fog. The quiet of the Nexus was almost eerie after the chaos of the battle, and the glowing crystal at the center of the void pulsed with a steady rhythm, as if it too was catching its breath.

Alara's mind was still racing, her thoughts swirling like the remnants of the storm that had torn through them. They had won—they had defeated Veridian, saved the Nexus from falling into his hands—but the victory felt hollow. The bond between her and Leo was more fragile than ever, and the cost of that bond weighed heavily on her heart.

Leo stirred in her arms, his eyes half-closed as he took a deep breath. "Alara," he murmured, his voice soft. "I can feel it... the bond is still there."

Alara nodded, brushing a strand of hair from his forehead. "I know. It's weaker now, but it's still there. We're still connected."

But for how long? The question hung in the air, unspoken but ever-present. The battle had strained the bond to its breaking point, and though they had survived, Alara knew that their connection could only withstand so much. The Nexus had fused them together in ways that defied the very laws of the universe, but it had also made them vulnerable.

"We need to understand this, Leo," she said quietly, her gaze drifting to the crystal at the heart of the Nexus. "We need to understand why the Nexus did this to us. What its purpose is."

Leo nodded, his eyes following hers to the glowing crystal. "You're right. The Nexus... it's more than just a machine. It's alive. It has a will of its own. And for some reason, it chose us."

Alara shivered at the thought. The Nexus had power beyond anything they could comprehend, but it had also shown them glimpses of something darker, something that lurked at the edges of time itself. The bond they shared was not just a random occurrence—it was part of a larger plan, a plan that they had only just begun to unravel.

"We need to go deeper," Alara said, her voice filled with determination. "We need to find the heart of the Nexus. If we can understand its purpose, maybe we can find a way to control this bond."

Leo's brow furrowed as he sat up, wincing from the lingering pain of the battle. "Deeper? Do you think there's more beyond this?"

Alara glanced around at the swirling void, the walls of time and space shifting and bending in ways that defied logic. "I don't know," she admitted. "But I can feel it. There's something... calling to us. Something deeper within the Nexus. We've only scratched the surface."

Leo hesitated for a moment, then nodded. "Okay. Let's do it. But we need to be careful, Alara. We barely made it through that last battle. If we push ourselves too hard..."

Alara placed her hand over his, offering him a reassuring smile. "I know. But we'll be careful. We'll figure this out, Leo. Together."

Leo's lips quirked into a small smile, and he squeezed her hand. "Together."

They rose to their feet, their bodies still aching from the fight, and began to move toward the center of the Nexus once more. The crystal at the heart of the Nexus pulsed with a steady rhythm, its light flickering like a heartbeat. Alara could feel the energy radiating from it, calling to her, drawing her in.

As they approached the crystal, the air around them seemed to thicken, the very fabric of reality growing more malleable. Time and space bent and twisted, and Alara felt a strange sensation in her chest, as if the bond between her and Leo was being pulled tighter, stretched to its limits.

"Do you feel that?" she asked, glancing at Leo.

He nodded, his expression grim. "Yeah. It's the bond. It's getting stronger."

Alara swallowed hard, her heart pounding in her chest. The bond was already fragile—if it grew any stronger, it might break under the strain. But they had no choice. They needed answers, and the only way to get them was to push forward.

They reached the crystal, and Alara placed her hand on its smooth surface. The moment her skin made contact, a shockwave of energy rippled through her body, and she gasped, her vision blurring as the world around her dissolved into a kaleidoscope of light and color.

Leo's hand found hers, and she could feel his presence beside her, grounding her, keeping her anchored as the Nexus pulled them deeper into its core.

The light grew brighter, more intense, and Alara felt herself being pulled into the heart of the crystal, the bond between her and Leo stretching tighter and tighter until it felt as though it might snap.

But then, just as suddenly as it had begun, the light faded, and they found themselves standing in a new chamber—a chamber that felt different from the rest of the Nexus. The air here was thick with energy, and the walls seemed to pulse with a faint, rhythmic hum.

"This place..." Leo whispered, his voice filled with awe. "It's... alive."

Alara nodded, her eyes wide as she took in their surroundings. This chamber was unlike anything they had seen before. It was vast, its walls lined with intricate patterns of light and shadow, and at the center of the room stood a large, glowing orb, its surface swirling with the same energy that filled the Nexus.

"This is it," Alara said, her voice trembling. "This is the heart of the Nexus."

They approached the orb cautiously, their steps slow and deliberate. The closer they got, the more Alara could feel the bond between them pulsing in sync with the orb, as if the Nexus itself was responding to their presence.

As they reached the orb, Alara extended her hand, hesitating for a moment before making contact. The moment her fingers touched the surface, the bond between her and Leo flared to life, and a flood of images and sensations filled her mind.

She saw timelines, endless possibilities, futures that stretched out before them like a web of light. She saw herself and Leo, standing at the center of it all, their bond the key to unlocking the power of the Nexus.

But with those visions came something darker—something that lurked at the edges of time, watching, waiting. It was the same darkness she had sensed before, the same presence that had haunted her visions.

"What is this?" Leo whispered, his voice filled with awe and fear.

Alara shook her head, her eyes wide as she stared at the swirling orb. "It's the Nexus. It's showing us... everything. The future. The past. All the timelines."

"But why?" Leo asked, his hand tightening around hers. "Why are we seeing this?"

Alara swallowed hard, her heart racing. "Because we're the key, Leo. The Nexus chose us for a reason. We're connected to it, to everything. And that means... we're responsible for it."

The weight of her words settled over them like a heavy blanket, and Leo's expression grew serious. "Responsible? For what?"

Alara took a deep breath, her gaze fixed on the swirling orb. "For time. For the Nexus. For everything that happens from here on out."

Leo's eyes widened, and he took a step back, his face pale. "Alara... I don't know if we're ready for that."

Alara's heart ached at the fear in his voice, but she knew that he was right. They weren't ready for this—for the responsibility that had been thrust upon them. But they didn't have a choice.

"We don't have a choice," she said softly. "The Nexus chose us, Leo. We have to figure out what it wants, what we're supposed to do."

Leo swallowed hard, his hand trembling in hers. "But what if we fail? What if we can't control this bond? What if..."

Alara squeezed his hand, her voice steady despite the fear that gnawed at her insides. "We won't fail. We'll figure this out, Leo. Together."

Leo's eyes softened, and he nodded, though the fear in his gaze remained. "Together," he repeated.

They stood in silence for a moment, the weight of their newfound responsibility heavy on their shoulders. The Nexus had given them a gift, but it had also given them a burden—one that they couldn't afford to ignore.

"We need to go deeper," Alara said, her voice firm. "There's more to this than what we've seen. We need to understand the full extent of what the Nexus is, what it wants from us."

Leo nodded, his expression grim. "I'm with you. Whatever happens, I'm with you."

As they stood before the glowing orb at the heart of the Nexus, Alara could feel the weight of the timelines pressing in around her. The images that had flooded her mind moments before still lingered in her thoughts—endless possibilities, futures that were yet to be written, and the darkness that seemed to loom at the edges of it all.

She tightened her grip on Leo's hand, drawing strength from their bond. The energy that connected them felt stronger than ever, pulsing in rhythm with the Nexus itself. But there was a fragility to it, as though the weight of the Nexus's power could shatter it at any moment.

"We need to understand this, Leo," Alara whispered, her eyes locked on the swirling orb before them. "We need to know why the Nexus chose us. Why it connected us like this."

Leo nodded, his expression serious. "I know. But it feels like every answer we get just leads to more questions."

Alara sighed softly, her mind racing as she tried to make sense of everything they had learned. The Nexus had tied them together, bound their fates in ways they still didn't fully understand. But why? What purpose did it serve?

"It has to be connected to the timelines," Alara said after a moment, her voice thoughtful. "The Nexus showed us all those possibilities—futures that could happen, but haven't yet. Maybe we're meant to… guide them somehow."

Leo's brow furrowed as he considered her words. "Guide them? Like, choose which future happens?"

"Maybe," Alara replied, though even as she said it, she knew it wasn't the full answer. "Or maybe it's something more than that. The Nexus is a conduit for time, but it's also alive. It has a will of its own, and for some reason, it's tied that will to us."

"But why us?" Leo asked, his frustration clear in his voice. "Why not someone else?"

Alara shook her head, the question gnawing at her. She didn't know why the Nexus had chosen them, but the bond they shared was no accident. It was part of something much larger, something they were only beginning to understand.

"We'll figure it out," Alara said softly, her gaze returning to the orb. "But we have to go deeper. There's more to this than what we've seen."

Leo hesitated for a moment, then nodded. "Okay. But we need to be careful. Whatever's down there… it's not going to be easy."

Alara nodded, her resolve hardening. They had come too far to turn back now. Together, they would face whatever lay ahead.

They stepped forward, their hands still intertwined, and as they moved closer to the orb, the air around them seemed to hum with anticipation. The energy of the Nexus pulsed in time with their heartbeats, drawing them deeper into its core.

As they reached the orb, the surface of the glowing structure rippled, and Alara felt a strange sensation wash over her—a pull, as though the Nexus itself was guiding her toward something just beyond her reach.

Without hesitation, she placed her hand on the orb once more, and the world around them shifted.

The chamber dissolved into a swirl of light and shadow, and Alara and Leo found themselves standing in what appeared to be a vast, endless expanse. The ground beneath their feet was solid, but the sky above them was a swirling mass of color and energy, the very fabric of time stretched out before them like an open canvas.

"This place…" Leo whispered, his voice filled with awe. "What is this?"

Alara shook her head, her eyes wide as she took in their surroundings. "I don't know. But it feels... different. Like we're not just inside the Nexus anymore."

They walked forward cautiously, the ground beneath them rippling with each step. The energy in the air was palpable, humming with a power that seemed to resonate with the bond between them.

As they ventured deeper into the expanse, Alara began to notice something strange. The timelines that had once swirled around them were now more focused, more tangible. She could see them stretching out into the distance—threads of light and shadow that connected to the futures they had glimpsed earlier.

But there was something else too. Something darker.

At the edges of the expanse, just beyond the reach of the light, there was a shadow—an ominous presence that sent a chill down Alara's spine.

"Leo," she said softly, her voice trembling. "Do you see that?"

Leo followed her gaze, his eyes narrowing as he spotted the shadow. "Yeah. I see it."

Alara's heart raced as she took a step back, her instincts screaming at her to run. But she couldn't. Not yet.

"We have to find out what that is," she said, her voice filled with determination. "It's connected to the Nexus somehow. And I think... I think it's connected to us."

Leo hesitated, his expression conflicted. "Alara, I don't like this. Whatever that thing is, it's dangerous."

"I know," Alara replied, her heart pounding in her chest. "But we have to understand it. We have to know what we're dealing with."

Leo's jaw tightened, but he nodded. "Okay. But we do this together."

Alara smiled, though the fear in her chest still lingered. "Always."

They moved cautiously toward the edge of the expanse, the shadow growing larger with each step. The air grew colder, the energy around them more erratic, and Alara could feel the bond between her and Leo pulsing in time with the darkness.

As they approached, the shadow began to take shape. It was massive, a towering figure that seemed to stretch out into infinity, its form shifting and twisting with the energy of the Nexus.

Alara's breath caught in her throat as she realized what it was. "It's a... Timekeeper," she whispered, her voice filled with awe and fear.

The Timekeepers were ancient beings, guardians of the Nexus who had long been thought to exist only in legend. They were said to be the protectors of time itself, beings of immense power who could bend reality to their will.

But this Timekeeper was different. Its presence was dark, its energy malevolent. It didn't feel like a protector—it felt like a threat.

Leo's eyes widened as he took a step back. "What do we do?"

Alara swallowed hard, her mind racing. The Timekeeper wasn't just a guardian—it was a manifestation of the Nexus's will. And if it had appeared now, it meant that something was very wrong.

"We need to talk to it," Alara said, her voice trembling. "We need to understand why it's here."

Leo stared at her in disbelief. "Talk to it? Are you serious?"

Alara nodded, though her heart pounded in her chest. "It's part of the Nexus, Leo. It's connected to everything. If we can understand it, maybe we can figure out what's happening to us."

Leo hesitated, then nodded. "Okay. But be careful."

Alara took a deep breath and stepped forward, her eyes locked on the towering figure before her. The air around her crackled with energy, and she could feel the weight of the Nexus pressing down on her, the bond between her and Leo pulsing in time with the shadow's movements.

"Timekeeper," she called out, her voice steady despite the fear that gripped her. "We are connected to the Nexus. We seek to understand our bond. Why has the Nexus tied us together?"

For a moment, there was only silence. The shadow loomed over them, its form shifting and twisting with the energy of the Nexus. And then, slowly, it spoke.

"You are the chosen," the Timekeeper said, its voice deep and resonant, like the sound of mountains shifting. "The Nexus has bound you together because you are the key. The key to its survival… and its destruction."

Alara's heart raced as the weight of the Timekeeper's words settled over her. "What do you mean? What are we supposed to do?"

The Timekeeper's form shifted again, its shadowy figure growing darker. "The Nexus is alive, but it is also dying. Its power has grown too great, and it cannot sustain itself. You are the only ones who can restore balance… or let it fall."

Alara's breath caught in her throat. The Nexus was dying? How could that be possible? It was the source of time itself, the very fabric of the universe. If it were to fall, the consequences would be unimaginable.

"We… we don't know how to fix it," Alara said, her voice trembling. "We don't know how to restore balance."

The Timekeeper's gaze seemed to pierce through her, and for a moment, Alara felt as though the weight of the entire universe was pressing down on her.

"You will learn," the Timekeeper said. "But know this: the bond between you and your companion is both your greatest strength... and your greatest weakness. If you are not careful, it will destroy you both."

Alara's mind raced as the Timekeeper's words echoed in her thoughts. The bond between her and Leo was the key to everything—the key to saving the Nexus, but also the key to their downfall. If they weren't careful, they would lose themselves in the power of the Nexus, consumed by the very force that had brought them together.

Leo stepped forward, his hand reaching for hers. "We'll figure this out, Alara," he said softly, his voice steady. "We'll save the Nexus. And we'll save each other."

Alara looked into his eyes and saw the same determination that burned within her. They were in this together, and no matter what lay ahead, they would face it as one.

She nodded, her resolve hardening. "Together."

The Timekeeper's presence loomed over them, a manifestation of the Nexus's power, its form shifting and twisting with an energy that felt as old as time itself. Alara's heart raced as she tried to comprehend what the ancient being had told them. The Nexus was dying, and somehow, she and Leo were at the center of it all—tied to the fate of the universe itself.

"We can't let it fall," Alara whispered, her voice barely audible. "If the Nexus collapses... everything collapses with it."

Leo's hand tightened around hers, his expression grim but resolute. "Then we figure out how to stop it. We've come too far to let it end like this."

Alara glanced at him, feeling the strength of his determination through their bond. She could sense his fear too—fear of the unknown, fear of losing her, fear of the power they had yet to fully understand. But beneath it all was an unwavering resolve, the same resolve that had carried them through every challenge they had faced together.

The Timekeeper's form shifted again, its voice echoing through the void. "The Nexus's power is vast, but it is also fragile. It has grown beyond its capacity to sustain itself, and now it teeters on the edge of collapse. You are the key to restoring balance... but the path ahead will not be easy."

Alara swallowed hard, the weight of the Timekeeper's words pressing down on her. "What do we need to do?"

The shadowy figure tilted its head, its gaze fixed on her. "The bond you share with your companion is both your greatest strength and your greatest weakness. It ties you to the Nexus, but it also leaves you vulnerable. If the bond is broken... you will fall, and so will the Nexus."

Alara's chest tightened as she processed the implications of the Timekeeper's warning. The bond between her and Leo had been forged by the Nexus, a connection that transcended time and space. But if that bond were to break, if one of them were to fall...

"We can't let that happen," Leo said, his voice steady. "We've come too far. We won't let the Nexus fall."

The Timekeeper's form flickered, its shadowy figure growing darker. "There is a way to restore balance, but it will require great sacrifice. The Nexus's power must be contained, its energy stabilized. Only then can it continue to exist without tearing itself apart."

Alara felt a chill run down her spine. "Sacrifice? What kind of sacrifice?"

The Timekeeper was silent for a moment, its form shifting as though it were considering its next words carefully. "The Nexus feeds on the energy of time, but it has grown too large, too powerful. It must be anchored, its power grounded in something... or someone. One of you must become the anchor, bound to the Nexus for all eternity."

Alara's breath caught in her throat as the weight of the Timekeeper's words settled over her. "Bound to the Nexus? What do you mean?"

"The Nexus must draw its energy from a living source," the Timekeeper explained. "One of you must remain within the Nexus, your essence tied to its core. In doing so, you will stabilize its power, allowing it to continue to exist. But it will come at a cost. You will no longer be able to leave. You will be bound to the Nexus, forever connected to its flow of time."

Leo's face paled, and Alara could feel the shock and fear radiating from him through their bond. "That's not an option," he said, his voice firm. "There has to be another way."

The Timekeeper's gaze remained fixed on them. "There is no other way. The Nexus's power is too great to be left unchecked. Without an anchor, it will continue to expand until it consumes everything. The choice is yours, but know that if you do nothing, the Nexus will collapse... and time itself will fall with it."

Alara's mind raced, her heart pounding in her chest. The choice before them was impossible—either one of them had to sacrifice themselves to save the Nexus, or they would both fall, along with everything they had fought to protect.

"We can't..." Leo's voice trailed off, his expression filled with anguish. "Alara, there has to be another way."

But even as he said it, Alara knew the truth. The Timekeeper was right. The Nexus was on the brink of collapse, and the only way to save it was for one of them to become its anchor, bound to the flow of time for eternity.

"I'll do it," Alara said softly, her voice steady despite the fear that gripped her heart.

Leo's head snapped toward her, his eyes wide with shock. "No. Alara, you can't—"

"I have to," she interrupted, her gaze locking with his. "Leo, if we don't do this, everything will be lost. The Nexus, the timelines, everything. We can't let that happen."

Leo's jaw clenched, his hands trembling as he shook his head. "There has to be another way. We'll find it. We always do."

Alara's heart ached at the pain in his voice, but she knew that there was no other option. The Nexus was too unstable, its power too great. If they didn't act now, there would be nothing left to save.

"It's the only way," she whispered, her voice filled with determination. "We'll still be connected, Leo. Even if I'm bound to the Nexus, we'll still have the bond. We'll still have each other."

Leo's eyes filled with tears as he stepped forward, his hands gripping her shoulders tightly. "I can't lose you, Alara. Not like this."

"You won't lose me," she said, her voice trembling with emotion. "We're connected, remember? No matter what happens, we'll always be connected."

Leo's hands tightened around hers, his eyes filled with desperation. "I don't want to do this without you."

Alara swallowed hard, her heart breaking at the sight of his pain. But she knew what had to be done. The Nexus had chosen her for a reason, and now it was time to fulfill that destiny.

"I love you, Leo," she whispered, her voice filled with resolve. "I always will. But we have to save the Nexus. We have to save time itself."

Leo's lips quivered as he tried to speak, but no words came. Instead, he pulled her into his arms, holding her tightly as though he could protect her from the fate that awaited her.

For a long moment, they stood there, wrapped in each other's embrace, their hearts beating in perfect sync. The bond between them pulsed with a warmth that filled Alara with strength, and for the first time since they had entered the Nexus, she felt at peace.

Finally, Leo pulled back, his eyes filled with tears. "I love you, Alara. More than anything."

Alara smiled through her own tears, her hand reaching up to cup his cheek. "I love you too. Always."

With one last, lingering kiss, Alara turned to face the Timekeeper. Her heart pounded in her chest, but her resolve was unshaken. She was ready.

The Timekeeper extended its hand, and the energy of the Nexus swirled around her, wrapping her in its embrace. Alara felt the bond between her and Leo pulsing stronger than ever, a lifeline that would carry her through the eternity that awaited her.

"You are the anchor," the Timekeeper said, its voice resonating through the void. "The Nexus will live through you."

Alara closed her eyes as the energy of the Nexus flowed through her, its power vast and overwhelming. But even as it filled her, she could still feel Leo's presence beside her, their bond unbroken.

No matter what happened, they would always be connected. And that was enough.

Alara's body felt weightless as the Nexus's energy wrapped around her, binding her to its core. She could feel the flow of time pulsing through her veins, the timelines stretching out before her like threads in a vast web. Every moment, every possibility, was hers to see, hers to guide.

But even as the power of the Nexus consumed her, she could still feel Leo's heartbeat echoing in her chest, the bond between them stronger than ever. They were connected, bound together by a force that transcended time and space.

"Alara," Leo's voice echoed in her mind, soft and filled with love. "We'll figure this out. We'll find a way to be together again."

Alara smiled, her heart swelling with warmth. "I know," she whispered. "We always do."

The Nexus pulsed around her, a living entity that thrived on the energy of time itself. Alara had become its anchor, its heart, but she was not alone. Leo was with her, his presence a constant source of strength and comfort.

They had saved the Nexus, but the journey was far from over. The bond between them would carry them through whatever lay ahead, guiding them through the endless possibilities of time.

Together, they would face the future. And no matter what the Nexus had in store for them, they would face it as one.

The Nexus pulsed steadily around Alara, and in that moment, she felt its energy woven into the very fabric of her being. She had become more than just a traveler through time—she had become part of it. But even as the Nexus anchored her to its power, her thoughts were consumed by Leo.

The weight of her decision hung heavily in the air, and though she stood before the swirling energy of the Nexus, something within her told her this was only the beginning. The Timekeeper's words echoed in her mind, a constant reminder of the path she had chosen. She was the anchor now, and that role came with responsibilities beyond anything she could have imagined.

Leo stepped forward, his hand trembling as he reached for her. The bond between them pulsed faintly, a fragile connection that felt as though it could be severed at any moment. But Alara could still feel him—his warmth, his strength, his unwavering presence.

"You're not doing this alone," Leo said softly, his voice filled with determination. "No matter what the Timekeeper says. We'll find a way to make it work."

Alara looked into his eyes, and for a moment, the weight of their situation seemed to fade. She believed him—she had to believe him. They had faced impossible odds before, and together, they had always found a way through. But this... this was different. The bond they shared was now intricately tied to the very core of the Nexus. It wasn't just their fates that were at stake—it was the fate of time itself.

"I don't know how we'll manage this, Leo," Alara whispered, her voice trembling. "But I won't lose you. I can't."

Leo's hand tightened around hers, his touch grounding her in the midst of the swirling chaos that surrounded them. "We'll figure it out, Alara. We have to."

As they stood there, Alara felt the energy of the Nexus shifting around them, almost as if it were alive—watching, waiting. The Timekeeper remained silent, its form now barely visible, a shadow in the distance. But Alara could feel its presence, like a constant hum at the back of her mind.

"What do we do now?" Leo asked, his brow furrowed as he glanced around the vast expanse of the Nexus.

Alara took a deep breath, her mind racing. "We need to understand the full extent of what's happened. The Nexus tied us together for a reason, but I don't think we've seen everything yet."

Leo nodded, his eyes narrowing in determination. "Then we keep going. We find out what the Nexus really wants from us."

They began to walk, their steps slow and measured as they ventured deeper into the heart of the Nexus. The walls around them shimmered with a strange, otherworldly light, and Alara could feel the pull of the timelines growing stronger with every step. It was as though the Nexus itself was guiding them, leading them toward something—some truth that lay hidden within its core.

As they moved, the bond between them pulsed steadily, its presence both comforting and unnerving. Alara could feel Leo's thoughts brushing against her own, his emotions weaving through her like a thread that tied them together. But there was something else too—something darker. A weight, a presence that lingered at the edge of her awareness, like a shadow that refused to fully reveal itself.

"Do you feel that?" Leo asked, his voice barely above a whisper.

Alara nodded, her gaze scanning their surroundings. "Yes. It's like… we're being watched."

Leo frowned, his hand tightening around hers. "I don't like it. This place is alive, Alara. It's more than just a conduit for time—it's sentient."

Alara's heart raced as she considered his words. The Nexus had always felt alive to her, but now, standing at the heart of its power, she realized just how true that was. The Nexus wasn't just a machine—it was a living entity, and they were connected to it in ways that defied explanation.

"Whatever it is," Alara said softly, "we need to understand it. We need to know what's waiting for us."

They continued walking, the energy around them growing more intense with each step. The air felt thick, charged with the weight of countless timelines converging in one place. And then, just as they reached the center of the chamber, the ground beneath them began to tremble.

Alara's heart leaped into her throat as she stumbled, her hand gripping Leo's for support. The walls of the Nexus shimmered, the light growing brighter and more erratic, as though the very fabric of reality was beginning to unravel.

"Leo!" Alara shouted, her voice barely audible over the roaring energy that now filled the air.

But before either of them could react, a shockwave of power surged through the chamber, knocking them both off their feet. Alara hit the ground hard, the breath knocked from her lungs as the world around her dissolved into a swirling vortex of light and sound.

For a moment, there was nothing but chaos—flashes of light, fragments of time, moments from the past, present, and future all colliding in a dizzying array of colors and images. Alara's mind raced, trying to make sense of the onslaught of sensations, but it was too much. She couldn't focus. She couldn't think.

And then, just as suddenly as it had begun, the chaos ceased.

Alara gasped, her chest heaving as she struggled to catch her breath. She blinked rapidly, her vision slowly coming back into focus, and when it did, she found herself lying on the floor of the Nexus, the air still and quiet around her.

"Leo?" she called out, her voice hoarse.

There was no response.

Panic surged through her as she scrambled to her feet, her eyes scanning the chamber for any sign of him. "Leo!" she shouted again, louder this time.

Still nothing.

Her heart pounded in her chest as she ran forward, her mind racing. The bond—she could still feel it, faint but present. He was alive.

He had to be. But the connection was weaker now, more fragile, as though something had torn them apart.

"Leo!" she screamed, her voice echoing through the chamber.

And then, at last, she heard it—a faint groan, barely audible but unmistakable.

Alara's breath caught in her throat as she followed the sound, her feet moving faster as she rounded a corner. And there, lying motionless on the ground, was Leo.

"Leo!" Alara dropped to her knees beside him, her hands trembling as she reached out to touch his face. His skin was pale, his breathing shallow, but he was alive.

"Leo," she whispered, her voice breaking. "Please... wake up."

For a long moment, there was no response, and Alara's heart sank. But then, slowly, Leo's eyes fluttered open.

"Alara..." he murmured, his voice barely more than a breath.

Alara let out a sob of relief, her hands cupping his face as tears streamed down her cheeks. "You're okay," she whispered. "You're okay."

Leo smiled weakly, his hand reaching up to brush a tear from her cheek. "I'm not going anywhere," he whispered. "We're still connected."

Alara nodded, her heart swelling with love and relief. The bond between them was still there—fragile, but unbroken.

"We have to keep moving," she said softly, her voice trembling with emotion. "We have to figure out what's happening here."

Leo nodded, his strength slowly returning as he pushed himself to his feet. "I'm with you."

Together, they stood at the heart of the Nexus, the energy of the timelines swirling around them like a storm. But despite the chaos,

Alara could feel a sense of purpose building within her. The Nexus had tied them together for a reason, and now it was up to them to understand why.

As they ventured deeper into the Nexus, the walls around them began to shift, the light growing dimmer as the energy became more erratic. Alara could feel the weight of the timelines pressing in on her, each one vying for her attention, pulling her in different directions.

"Alara," Leo said, his voice strained. "Something's happening. The bond—it's changing."

Alara's breath caught in her throat as she felt it too. The bond between them was shifting, growing stronger and weaker in waves, as though the very fabric of their connection was being stretched and pulled in different directions.

"It's the Nexus," Alara said, her voice filled with realization. "It's testing us. It's pushing us to our limits."

Leo frowned, his brow furrowed in concentration. "But why? What does it want?"

Alara shook her head, her mind racing. "I don't know. But I think... I think it's trying to show us something."

They continued walking, the air around them growing thicker with energy. Alara could feel the pull of the Nexus growing stronger, drawing her deeper into its core. And then, just as they reached the center of the chamber, the ground beneath them began to tremble again.

This time, however, Alara was ready.

"Hold on!" she shouted, her hand gripping Leo's as the energy of the Nexus surged around them.

The walls shimmered, the light flickering in and out of focus, and Alara could feel the timelines converging around them, each one pulling at her, begging for her attention.

"Alara!" Leo shouted, his voice barely audible over the roaring energy.

"I'm here!" she called back, her voice filled with determination. "Stay with me!"

The bond between them pulsed stronger than ever, a lifeline that tethered them together in the chaos. Alara could feel Leo's presence beside her, his strength, his love, and she knew that no matter what happened, they would face it together.

The Nexus roared around them, the energy reaching a fever pitch as Alara and Leo held on to each other, tethered by the fragile bond that connected their souls. Alara could feel the timelines twisting and bending, fragments of the past, present, and future colliding in a chaotic storm. It felt like the very fabric of reality was unraveling before their eyes, and for a brief moment, Alara wondered if they would be consumed by the Nexus entirely.

But then, through the noise and chaos, something shifted. The energy around them began to stabilize, the erratic pulses of light and sound softening into a steady rhythm. Alara felt a strange sense of calm wash over her, as though the Nexus was guiding them, showing them the way forward.

"We're close," Alara whispered, her voice trembling. "I can feel it."

Leo nodded, his hand gripping hers tightly. "Whatever it is, we're not turning back now."

They took a step forward, and the air around them shimmered, the timelines shifting as though they were parting to reveal something hidden within. Alara's breath caught in her throat as a new vision unfolded before her eyes—an image of the future, clearer than any she had seen before.

In this future, she saw herself standing at the center of the Nexus, the glowing orb before her pulsing with an intense, otherworldly light. But she was not alone. Beside her stood Leo, his hand resting on the orb as the energy of the Nexus flowed through them both. They were connected, not just to each other but to the Nexus itself, their bond intertwined with the very fabric of time.

"We're the key," Alara whispered, her voice filled with awe. "The Nexus… it needs us."

Leo's brow furrowed in confusion. "What do you mean?"

Alara closed her eyes, the vision still fresh in her mind. "The Nexus is more than just a machine. It's alive, and it's been waiting for us. We're the ones who can stabilize it, who can keep it from collapsing."

"But how?" Leo asked, his voice filled with uncertainty. "How can we possibly do that?"

Alara shook her head, her mind racing as she tried to make sense of the overwhelming flood of information. "I don't know yet, but the bond between us… it's the key. The Nexus tied us together for a reason. We're part of its design."

As they continued walking, the air grew warmer, and the light around them began to shift once more, revealing a massive structure in the distance. The walls of the Nexus stretched up into the sky, towering over them like the remnants of an ancient city. The energy here was palpable, pulsing with a life force that made Alara's skin tingle.

"This is it," Leo said softly, his voice barely more than a breath. "The heart of the Nexus."

Alara nodded, her eyes wide as she took in the sight before her. The heart of the Nexus was unlike anything she had ever seen—a massive crystalline structure, glowing with an ethereal light that seemed to pulse in rhythm with the very beat of time itself. It was beautiful, but there was something else too—something dangerous.

"We have to be careful," Alara said, her voice filled with caution. "The Nexus is powerful, and if we make the wrong move…"

Leo nodded, his expression serious. "I know. But we've come too far to stop now."

Together, they approached the crystalline structure, the air around them growing thick with energy. Alara could feel the pull of the Nexus stronger than ever, as though it were calling to her, urging her to take the next step. But as she reached out, a sudden wave of nausea washed over her, and she stumbled, her hand clutching her chest as the bond between her and Leo flared with an intensity that made her gasp.

"Alara!" Leo shouted, rushing to her side.

"I'm okay," she said, her voice shaky as she steadied herself. "It's the bond. The Nexus… it's amplifying it."

Leo frowned, his hand resting on her shoulder. "But why? What's it trying to do?"

Alara took a deep breath, her mind still reeling from the onslaught of sensations. "It's trying to merge us with the Nexus. It wants to make us part of it, to tie us to its power permanently."

Leo's eyes widened in shock. "But if we let that happen, won't we lose ourselves? Won't we become… part of the Nexus?"

Alara nodded, her heart pounding in her chest. "Yes. If we allow the bond to grow too strong, we'll be consumed by the Nexus. We'll no longer be separate—we'll be one with it."

Leo's hand tightened around hers, his face pale. "We can't let that happen."

"No," Alara agreed, her voice firm. "But we have to find a way to stabilize the Nexus without letting it consume us. If we don't, everything will fall apart."

They stood there in silence for a moment, the weight of their situation pressing down on them like a heavy fog. The bond between them pulsed faintly, a reminder of the power that tied them together, but also of the danger they faced.

"We'll find a way," Leo said, his voice filled with determination. "We always do."

Alara smiled weakly, though the fear still gnawed at her insides. She wanted to believe him, wanted to believe that they could face this challenge like they had faced all the others. But the Nexus was different. It was alive, sentient, and its power was beyond anything they had ever encountered.

Taking a deep breath, Alara stepped forward, her hand hovering just above the surface of the crystalline structure. She could feel the energy of the Nexus swirling around her, tugging at the bond between her and Leo, urging her to give in to its power.

But she resisted. With every ounce of strength she had, she resisted.

As her hand touched the surface, a wave of light washed over her, and the world around them shifted once more. They were no longer standing at the heart of the Nexus—instead, they found themselves in a vast, empty void, the only light coming from the faint glow of the bond that connected them.

"Where are we?" Leo asked, his voice filled with confusion.

Alara shook her head, her eyes scanning the void. "I don't know. But this... this feels like a test."

Leo frowned. "A test? Of what?"

Alara's gaze focused on the bond between them, the faint glow that pulsed in time with their heartbeats. "Of us. Of the bond."

They stood there in silence for what felt like an eternity, the void around them empty and still. But then, slowly, figures began to emerge from the darkness—shadowy forms that took shape before their eyes, their faces familiar but distant.

Alara's breath caught in her throat as she recognized the figures. They were reflections of herself and Leo, but from different timelines—alternate versions of who they could have been, who they might still become.

"These are... us," Leo whispered, his voice filled with awe. "But from different futures."

Alara nodded, her heart racing as the figures moved closer. "The Nexus is showing us what could happen. These are the timelines that depend on us."

One by one, the figures began to speak, their voices soft but clear, each one offering a glimpse into a possible future. In some, Alara and Leo stood together, their bond stronger than ever, guiding the Nexus to stability and peace. In others, they were torn apart, their connection severed by the overwhelming power of the Nexus, leaving chaos in their wake.

But the darkest future of all was the one where they allowed the Nexus to consume them entirely, their identities lost as they became one with the flow of time, trapped in an eternal loop of existence with no way out.

"We can't let that happen," Leo said, his voice trembling. "We can't let ourselves become part of the Nexus."

Alara swallowed hard, her mind racing. "We have to choose, Leo. We have to decide which path to take."

But the choice wasn't simple. Every future came with its own set of risks, its own set of sacrifices. And no matter what they chose, there would be consequences.

"We need to stabilize the Nexus," Alara said, her voice filled with resolve. "But we can't let it control us. We have to find a way to guide it without losing ourselves in the process."

Leo nodded, though his face was pale with fear. "And how do we do that?"

Alara closed her eyes, the bond between them pulsing stronger than ever. "We trust each other. We trust the bond."

The figures around them began to fade, their voices growing quieter as they retreated into the darkness. But the message they had delivered remained clear—Alara and Leo were the key to everything. The bond they shared was their greatest strength, but also their greatest risk.

"We can't let fear control us," Alara whispered, her voice steady. "We've been chosen for this, Leo. The Nexus trusts us. We just have to trust ourselves."

Leo's hand tightened around hers, his voice filled with determination. "Then let's finish this. Together."

The bond between Alara and Leo pulsed steadily as they stood together in the void, their fingers intertwined as if to remind themselves that they still had each other, that despite everything they faced, they were not alone. The figures of their alternate selves had faded into the darkness, leaving behind only the weight of the choices that lay ahead.

Alara's heart pounded in her chest as she stared at the faint glow of their bond, the light shimmering in the empty space around them. The Nexus was still alive, still watching, and it had placed the fate of time itself in their hands. The responsibility was overwhelming, almost suffocating, but Alara knew they couldn't turn back now.

"We have to choose," Leo said softly, his voice breaking the heavy silence. "We have to decide what kind of future we want."

Alara nodded, her mind racing as she considered the paths that lay before them. Every choice carried immense consequences, not just for them but for the entire universe. If they allowed the Nexus to consume them, to merge their identities into the flow of time, they might stabilize it, but they would lose themselves in the process. On the other hand, if they tried to control the Nexus without fully understanding its power, they risked causing it to collapse, plunging the timelines into chaos.

The darkness at the edges of the Nexus felt closer than ever, as though it were waiting for them to falter, to make the wrong choice.

"We need to find balance," Alara said, her voice firm. "The Nexus wants to tie us to it, but we can't let it control us. We have to guide it, not the other way around."

Leo's eyes met hers, and she could see the same determination mirrored in his gaze. "But how do we do that? How do we control something as powerful as the Nexus without losing ourselves in the process?"

Alara took a deep breath, her thoughts swirling. "We have to focus on the bond. That's the key. The Nexus tied us together for a reason—it's using our connection to stabilize itself. But if we stay grounded, if we hold on to who we are, we can use that bond to guide the Nexus without letting it consume us."

Leo frowned, his brow furrowed in concentration. "You think that's possible?"

Alara nodded, though the uncertainty still gnawed at her. "It has to be. The Nexus is powerful, but it's not invincible. It needs us just as much as we need it. If we can keep control of the bond, we can keep control of the Nexus."

Leo's grip on her hand tightened, his voice filled with resolve. "Then we do this together."

Alara smiled, though the weight of their task still loomed large in her mind. Together. That was the one thing she was sure of—no matter what happened, no matter how dark the path ahead might become, they would face it together.

The void around them shimmered, and slowly, the space began to shift, the darkness giving way to the swirling light of the Nexus once more. The crystalline structure at the heart of the Nexus pulsed faintly in the distance, its glow beckoning them forward.

Alara took a step toward it, the energy of the Nexus flowing through her like a current. She could feel its pull, the immense power that radiated from it, but she held on to Leo's hand, grounding herself in their connection.

"We have to stabilize it," she said softly, her voice barely audible over the hum of the Nexus. "But we can't let it take control."

Leo nodded, his eyes fixed on the glowing crystal. "Then let's do this."

They approached the heart of the Nexus, the air around them growing thick with energy. Alara's skin tingled as the power of the timelines swirled around her, but she remained focused, her thoughts centered on the bond that tied her to Leo.

The crystal pulsed as they drew near, its light flickering like a heartbeat. Alara could feel the weight of the Nexus pressing down on her, its energy probing at the edges of her consciousness, searching for a way in. But she resisted. She wouldn't let it take control.

"Leo," she whispered, her voice trembling. "Are you ready?"

Leo's hand tightened around hers, his eyes locked on the crystal. "I'm with you, Alara. No matter what happens, we'll do this together."

Alara nodded, her heart pounding in her chest. Together. That was all that mattered.

With a deep breath, Alara reached out toward the crystal, her hand trembling as she made contact. The moment her fingers touched the surface, a surge of energy rushed through her, and for a brief moment, she felt as though she were being pulled into the very heart of the Nexus. But she held on—held on to Leo, held on to the bond that connected them.

The energy swirled around her, growing more intense with each passing second, but Alara focused on the connection between her and Leo, using it as an anchor to keep herself grounded. She could feel the Nexus trying to pull her in, trying to merge her with its power, but she resisted.

"We have to stay grounded," she said, her voice strained. "We can't let it take control."

Leo's grip on her hand tightened, and Alara could feel his strength flowing through her, steadying her as the Nexus's power continued to build.

"We're stronger together," Leo said softly. "We won't let it take us."

The crystal pulsed again, and this time, Alara felt a shift in the energy around them. It was subtle at first, but as the seconds passed, she realized what was happening. The Nexus was responding to them—to the bond they shared. It was stabilizing.

"It's working," Alara whispered, her heart swelling with hope. "We're stabilizing the Nexus."

But just as the words left her mouth, something shifted. The air around them grew colder, and a dark presence began to seep into the chamber, like a shadow creeping in from the edges of the void.

Alara's heart raced as she glanced around, her eyes searching for the source of the darkness. And then, out of the shadows, it appeared.

Veridian.

His form was barely visible, a dark figure looming in the distance, but Alara could feel his presence like a weight pressing down on her chest.

"No," she whispered, her voice filled with dread. "It can't be."

But it was. Veridian had returned.

"Alara," Leo said, his voice filled with urgency. "We have to finish this before he gets here."

Alara nodded, her mind racing as she refocused on the crystal. They had to stabilize the Nexus before Veridian reached them, or everything they had fought for would be lost.

The crystal pulsed once more, and Alara could feel the bond between her and Leo growing stronger, amplifying their connection as they worked together to bring the Nexus under control.

But Veridian was getting closer. She could feel his presence, his hatred, like a storm building on the horizon. He wasn't just coming for the Nexus—he was coming for them.

"We have to hurry," Alara said, her voice trembling. "He's almost here."

Leo's face was pale, but his resolve never wavered. "We'll finish this, Alara. We have to."

They focused all their energy on the bond, on the connection that tied them together. The Nexus pulsed in response, the energy swirling around them as it stabilized, but Alara could feel the darkness closing in.

Veridian was almost upon them.

The air grew thick with tension as Veridian's presence loomed closer, the cold, dark energy radiating from him like a suffocating fog. Alara's heart pounded in her chest, her mind racing as she struggled to maintain control of the Nexus. Every second felt like an eternity, the weight of their task pressing down on her like a vice.

"Alara," Leo said, his voice strained. "We can't let him stop us."

Alara nodded, her hands trembling as she focused on the bond between them, using it to stabilize the Nexus. The crystal pulsed steadily beneath her fingers, but the strain of controlling such immense power was taking its toll.

"We're almost there," she whispered, her voice shaking. "Just a little more…"

But as they neared the point of stabilization, the darkness around them deepened. Veridian's shadowy form was now fully visible, his eyes burning with malice as he approached them, his steps slow and deliberate.

"You think you can control the Nexus?" Veridian sneered, his voice filled with contempt. "You're nothing. You're weak."

Alara's breath caught in her throat as Veridian's words pierced through her. For a brief moment, doubt crept into her mind. Could they really do this? Could they control something as powerful as the Nexus without losing themselves in the process?

But then, she felt it—the bond. Strong, steady, unbreakable. Leo's presence was with her, his strength flowing through her like a lifeline, grounding her in the midst of the chaos.

"We're not weak," Alara said, her voice filled with resolve. "We're stronger together."

Veridian's eyes narrowed, his expression twisting with rage. "Then I'll destroy you both."

The battle that followed was unlike anything they had faced before. Veridian's power was immense, fueled by the darkness that had consumed him, but Alara and Leo fought as one, their bond giving them the strength to hold their ground.

The Nexus pulsed around them, its energy surging with every strike, but Alara could feel the strain of the battle weighing heavily on her. The bond between her and Leo was their greatest strength, but it was also their greatest vulnerability. If Veridian managed to sever it, they would fall.

"We can't let him break the bond," Alara shouted, her voice filled with urgency. "It's the only thing keeping us connected to the Nexus."

Leo nodded, his face pale with exertion. "We won't let him."

Together, they unleashed the full force of the Nexus, their connection amplifying its power as they fought to stabilize it. The air crackled with energy, and Alara could feel the timelines shifting around them, bending to the will of the Nexus as they brought it under control.

But Veridian was relentless. He struck at them with everything he had, his attacks fueled by a hatred that seemed to know no bounds. Alara could feel the bond between her and Leo fraying at the edges, the strain of the battle threatening to tear them apart.

"Hold on!" Alara shouted, her voice trembling. "We're almost there!"

Leo gritted his teeth, his hand tightening around hers as they poured the last of their strength into the Nexus. The crystal pulsed brightly, the light growing stronger as the energy stabilized.

And then, with a final surge of power, the Nexus settled. The timelines fell into place, the chaos around them giving way to a calm, steady rhythm. They had done it.

The Nexus was stabilized.

The Nexus hummed with newfound stability, the swirling chaos of the timelines now flowing in perfect harmony. Alara and Leo stood at the heart of it all, their hands still intertwined, their hearts pounding in unison as the energy of the Nexus pulsed around them. They had done it—they had stabilized the Nexus. But the weight of what had just happened still lingered, heavy in the air.

Alara's chest rose and fell with labored breaths as she looked around the chamber, her eyes scanning the space for any sign of Veridian. The dark energy that had filled the room moments before had dissipated, but the memory of Veridian's presence still clung to her like a shadow.

"Is he... gone?" Leo asked, his voice hoarse from the strain of the battle.

Alara hesitated, her gaze sweeping over the chamber once more. "I don't know," she whispered, her heart still racing. "But I can't feel him anymore. It's like the Nexus pushed him out."

Leo let out a shaky breath, his grip on her hand loosening slightly. "We did it," he murmured, his voice filled with disbelief. "We actually did it."

Alara nodded, though the relief that should have come with their victory was tempered by the knowledge of the price they had paid.

The Nexus was stable, yes—but at what cost? Their bond, the connection that had tied them together from the beginning, had been stretched to its very limits. And though they had emerged victorious, Alara could feel that something had changed.

"We're not the same," Alara said softly, her eyes meeting Leo's. "The Nexus… it's still part of us."

Leo's expression grew somber as he nodded, his brow furrowed in thought. "I can feel it too. The bond between us—it's different now."

Alara swallowed hard, the realization sinking in. The bond that had once been a lifeline between them, a tether that kept them grounded, had become something more—something intertwined with the very fabric of the Nexus itself. They were no longer just connected to each other—they were connected to time, to the flow of the universe.

"What does that mean for us?" Leo asked, his voice filled with uncertainty.

Alara shook her head, her mind racing. "I don't know. But I think… I think it means we're part of the Nexus now. We're not just observers—we're part of the flow of time."

Leo's eyes widened, and Alara could see the fear in his gaze. "So… we're trapped here?"

Alara's heart clenched at the thought. Trapped. The word echoed in her mind, sending a chill down her spine. They had stabilized the Nexus, but in doing so, they had become part of it. They had anchored themselves to the very thing they had fought to control.

"I don't know," she said softly, her voice trembling. "But I can feel it, Leo. We're tied to this place now. We're part of the Nexus's balance."

Leo took a step back, his hand slipping from hers as he ran a hand through his hair. "But what does that mean for us? Can we leave? Can we go back?"

Alara's throat tightened as she tried to find the words to explain what she was feeling. The Nexus was no longer just a place—it was a part of them now. The bond that had connected them to each other had evolved into something far more complex, something that tied them to the very flow of time.

"I don't know," she repeated, her voice barely above a whisper. "But we're not the same, Leo. We're... different now."

Leo's jaw clenched, and Alara could see the conflict in his eyes. He wanted to believe that they could go back, that they could return to the lives they had left behind. But deep down, she knew that wasn't possible—not anymore.

"We have to find out what this means," Alara said, her voice filled with determination. "We have to understand the full extent of what we've done."

Leo nodded slowly, though his expression remained troubled. "But where do we even start?"

Alara glanced around the chamber, her gaze settling on the glowing crystal at the heart of the Nexus. The crystal pulsed faintly, its light softer now that the Nexus had been stabilized. But Alara could still feel its power—the energy of the timelines swirling around them like an invisible current.

"The Nexus is the key," she said, her voice steady. "We need to understand how it works, how it's tied to us. If we can figure that out, maybe we can find a way to control it without losing ourselves."

Leo frowned, his eyes narrowing in thought. "You think we can control it?"

Alara hesitated for a moment before nodding. "I think we have to. The Nexus isn't going away—it's part of us now. But if we can learn to control it, we can figure out how to live with it, how to use its power without being consumed by it."

Leo's expression softened, and he took her hand once more, his grip firm and reassuring. "Then we do it together."

Alara smiled, though the fear still lingered in the back of her mind. Together. That was the one thing she was sure of—no matter what happened, they would face it as one.

The days that followed were a blur of exploration and discovery as Alara and Leo delved deeper into the mysteries of the Nexus. The chamber at the heart of the Nexus became their home, a place where they could study the flow of time and learn to navigate the complex web of timelines that stretched out before them.

But as they delved deeper into the Nexus's power, they quickly realized that their bond was not the only thing that had changed. The Nexus had become an extension of themselves, a conduit through which they could access the flow of time. With a single thought, they could reach out and touch the timelines, bending them to their will.

At first, the power was intoxicating. Alara marveled at the ease with which they could manipulate time, shifting events and altering outcomes with a mere flick of their minds. It was as though they had been given the ability to reshape the very fabric of the universe, to control the course of history itself.

But with that power came a heavy responsibility. The more they used the Nexus's energy, the more they realized the dangers that came with it. Every change they made to the timelines had ripple effects, consequences that stretched far beyond what they could see.

"We have to be careful," Leo said one evening as they sat together at the heart of the Nexus, the glow of the crystal casting a soft light over their faces. "Every time we change something, we're altering the course of history. We could cause a chain reaction that we can't control."

Alara nodded, her thoughts heavy with the weight of their newfound power. "I know. But it's hard not to want to fix things, to make things better."

Leo sighed, his brow furrowed in thought. "I get it. But we can't fix everything. The timelines are too fragile. If we start messing with the flow of time too much, we'll break it."

Alara's heart ached at the truth of his words. They had been given a gift, a power beyond anything they could have imagined, but it came with limitations. The Nexus had tied them to the flow of time, but it had also bound them to its rules.

"We have to find balance," Alara said softly, her voice filled with resolve. "We can't let the power consume us."

Leo's gaze softened, and he reached out to take her hand. "We won't. We'll figure this out, Alara. Together."

As the days turned into weeks, Alara and Leo continued to study the Nexus, learning to navigate the intricate web of timelines and understanding the full extent of their bond. The Nexus had stabilized, but the connection between them and the flow of time remained, a constant presence that pulsed faintly in the back of their minds.

But even as they grew more comfortable with their new abilities, the weight of the Nexus's power never left them. The timelines stretched out before them, endless and ever-shifting, and Alara couldn't shake the feeling that something—someone—was watching them from the shadows.

"Do you ever feel like we're not alone?" Alara asked one evening as they sat together at the heart of the Nexus, the soft glow of the crystal illuminating the chamber.

Leo glanced at her, his brow furrowed in thought. "Sometimes. Why?"

Alara hesitated, her fingers tracing the surface of the crystal. "I don't know. It's just... the Nexus is alive, and it's tied to us now. I can't help but feel like there's something else here with us, something we haven't discovered yet."

Leo's expression grew serious, and he nodded slowly. "I've felt it too. Like a presence, just at the edge of my awareness."

Alara's heart raced as the feeling she had been trying to ignore resurfaced once more. The Nexus had stabilized, but that didn't mean the danger was over. There were still mysteries they hadn't uncovered, still shadows lurking in the corners of time.

"We need to be careful," Leo said, his voice filled with caution. "The Nexus may be stable now, but that doesn't mean it's safe."

Alara nodded, her gaze fixed on the glowing crystal before them. The Nexus had given them power beyond anything they could have imagined, but it had also tied them to a force they didn't fully understand.

And deep down, Alara knew that their journey was far from over.

As Alara sat beside Leo, her fingers tracing the smooth surface of the Nexus crystal, a soft hum filled the chamber. The energy of the timelines still pulsed faintly, but there was a tension in the air, as though something unseen was waiting just beyond their perception.

"I feel it too," Leo murmured, his voice barely above a whisper. "Like the Nexus is hiding something from us."

Alara's brow furrowed as she closed her eyes, focusing on the connection that tethered them to the Nexus. The bond between her and Leo pulsed steadily, a constant reminder of the power they now wielded. But beneath that familiar pulse, there was something else—something faint and distant, but growing stronger with every passing second.

"We need to go deeper," Alara said, her voice filled with resolve. "There's more to the Nexus than what we've seen. I can feel it."

Leo glanced at her, his expression conflicted. "Are you sure? We've barely scratched the surface, and the last time we pushed too hard…"

Alara's eyes flicked to the crystal, her heart pounding in her chest. "I know. But I think… I think there's something at the very heart of the Nexus, something we haven't uncovered yet. And I need to know what it is."

Leo hesitated for a moment, then nodded. "Alright. But we do this together."

With a deep breath, Alara placed her hand on the Nexus crystal, the familiar energy of the timelines surging through her like a current. Leo's hand found hers, and together, they reached out with their minds, delving deeper into the flow of time than they ever had before.

The chamber around them faded into a swirl of light and shadow, and Alara felt herself being pulled deeper into the core of the Nexus. The bond between her and Leo tightened, but instead of the comforting warmth she had come to rely on, there was a cold, distant presence—a presence that didn't belong to either of them.

And then, just as the swirling light reached its peak, they found themselves standing in a vast, dark void.

"Where are we?" Leo asked, his voice filled with uncertainty.

Alara's heart raced as she looked around, her eyes scanning the endless expanse of darkness. "I don't know... but something feels wrong."

As they took a step forward, a sudden chill washed over them, and from the shadows, a figure emerged—a figure that made Alara's blood run cold.

It was her.

But not the Alara she knew. This version of herself was cold, distant, her eyes devoid of the warmth and compassion that had defined her. She stood tall, cloaked in dark energy, and as her gaze locked with Alara's, a cruel smile spread across her face.

"Welcome to your future," the other Alara said, her voice cold and mocking. "This is what you become."

Alara's breath caught in her throat, her mind reeling from the shock. "What... what are you talking about?"

The other Alara stepped forward, her eyes gleaming with malice. "The Nexus chose you because it knew you would bend to its will. You've been walking this path since the moment you touched the crystal. And now, you've reached the end."

"No!" Alara shouted, her voice trembling with fear. "That's not true. We've been stabilizing the Nexus—we've been controlling it."

"Controlling it?" the other Alara laughed, the sound cold and bitter. "You've been feeding it. Every time you used its power, you gave it more control over you. And now, you're nothing more than a vessel—a conduit for the Nexus to shape the future as it sees fit."

Leo stepped forward, his hand still gripping Alara's tightly. "We won't let that happen. We're stronger together."

The other Alara's gaze shifted to Leo, her smile widening. "You think your bond can save you? It's already too late. The Nexus has been waiting for this moment—waiting for you to fully submit to its power. And now that you have… there's no turning back."

Alara's heart pounded in her chest as the full weight of the other Alara's words sank in. The Nexus had been manipulating them, guiding them toward this moment. Every choice they had made, every step they had taken, had been part of the Nexus's plan to consume them, to make them part of its eternal cycle.

"You're lying," Alara said, though her voice trembled with doubt.

The other Alara raised an eyebrow, her expression cold and calculating. "Am I? You've felt it, haven't you? The pull of the Nexus, the way it's been changing you. You've already lost control. And soon, you'll lose yourselves completely."

"No!" Leo shouted, his voice filled with defiance. "We won't let that happen."

The other Alara's smile faded, replaced by a look of cold indifference. "You don't have a choice."

And with that, she raised her hand, the dark energy of the Nexus swirling around her like a storm. The ground beneath Alara and Leo trembled, and the air crackled with the raw power of time itself.

Alara's breath hitched as the energy surged toward them, but in that moment, something within her snapped. The bond between her and Leo flared to life, stronger than ever, and Alara felt a surge of power rush through her—power that wasn't the Nexus's, but her own.

"No," Alara said, her voice steady and filled with resolve. "We choose our own fate."

With a single thought, Alara reached out to the bond, amplifying its strength and pushing back against the dark energy that surrounded them. The other Alara's eyes widened in shock as the energy recoiled, the power of the bond overpowering the Nexus's control.

"You can't stop this!" the other Alara screamed, her voice filled with rage. "You're already part of the Nexus!"

But Alara's eyes blazed with determination as she took a step forward, her hand still gripping Leo's tightly. "We make our own future. And we won't be controlled."

In a final burst of energy, Alara unleashed the full force of the bond, and the dark version of herself shattered into nothingness, her form dissolving into the void.

The chamber around them stabilized, the dark energy dissipating as the power of the Nexus receded. Alara and Leo stood together at the heart of the Nexus, their bond stronger than ever.

But as the silence settled over them, Alara couldn't shake the feeling that this was only the beginning.

The Nexus was stable—for now. But the darkness that had consumed her other self still lingered at the edges of her mind, a reminder that the power they wielded came with a cost.

And as they looked out over the endless expanse of timelines stretching before them, Alara knew one thing for certain: their journey was far from over.

Chapter - 19
The Veil Between Worlds

The silence that filled the Nexus was heavy, almost suffocating. Alara and Leo stood together, their hands still clasped, their hearts pounding from the intensity of what had just transpired. They had stabilized the Nexus, defeated Veridian's dark presence, and for a moment, it seemed like peace had returned.

But Alara knew better. The Nexus was not finished with them.

As the chamber around them began to fade, a strange sensation washed over Alara. It felt as though the world itself was unraveling beneath her feet, as if the very fabric of reality was being pulled apart. Her breath quickened as the ground beneath them shifted, and the familiar energy of the Nexus surged once more.

"Leo..." Alara whispered, her voice trembling. "Something's wrong."

Before Leo could respond, the world around them dissolved, and the Nexus chamber shattered into fragments of light and darkness. Alara's vision blurred, her body weightless as she was pulled into an endless void, the bond between her and Leo stretching thin, like a fragile thread on the verge of snapping.

"Alara!" Leo's voice echoed through the darkness, filled with panic.

"I'm here!" she called back, but her voice felt distant, swallowed by the void.

And then, just as suddenly as it had begun, the sensation stopped.

Alara's eyes fluttered open, her breath ragged as she took in her surroundings. She wasn't in the Nexus anymore. The chamber was gone, replaced by something far more unsettling.

She stood on the edge of an enormous cliff, overlooking a vast, barren landscape bathed in the light of a pale, cold sun. The ground beneath her was cracked and lifeless, stretching out in jagged formations that seemed to go on forever. There were no trees, no water—only the endless horizon of dust and decay.

But the most terrifying part was the sky. It was wrong.

Above her, the sky swirled with colors that defied explanation—shades of violet, crimson, and deep black, all blending together in a chaotic, swirling mass. It was as though the sky had been torn apart, revealing the churning, unstable forces of the universe beyond.

Alara's breath hitched in her throat as she stared at the swirling mass above. This wasn't any place she recognized. It wasn't even the Nexus. It was something else—something far worse.

"Leo?" Alara called out, her voice barely a whisper.

There was no response. The cold wind whipped through her hair, and for the first time since they had been connected, Alara couldn't feel Leo's presence. The bond, the lifeline that had tied them together through everything, was gone.

Panic surged through her chest as she took a step forward, her eyes scanning the endless wasteland for any sign of him. But there was nothing. Only the desolate landscape and the swirling, unnatural sky above.

"Leo!" she shouted again, louder this time, her voice cracking with desperation.

Still nothing.

A deep sense of dread settled in her stomach as the realization sank in. She was alone. Completely, utterly alone.

Her heart pounded in her chest as she tried to make sense of what had happened. One moment, she and Leo had been in the Nexus, victorious over Veridian. The next, she had been pulled into this strange, desolate world. But why? What had gone wrong?

As her mind raced for answers, a faint whisper echoed through the air, so soft that Alara almost missed it.

"Alara…"

Her breath caught in her throat as she spun around, her eyes wide with shock. The voice was familiar, hauntingly so. But it wasn't Leo.

"Who's there?" she demanded, her voice trembling.

The whisper came again, louder this time. "You cannot escape… you are bound to it."

Alara's heart raced as she turned in every direction, searching for the source of the voice. But the landscape around her was empty, barren. There was no one there.

And yet, she could feel it—something watching her, something ancient and powerful, lurking just beyond the edge of her perception. The feeling was suffocating, as though the air itself was alive with the presence of whatever had spoken to her.

"You are part of the Nexus now," the voice whispered again, sending a chill down her spine. "And the Nexus is part of you."

Alara's blood ran cold as the words sank in. The Nexus had stabilized, but in doing so, it had tied her to its power in ways she didn't fully understand. She and Leo had been connected to it, but now… now it felt as though the Nexus itself was inside her, a presence that pulsed in the back of her mind.

"I don't want this," Alara whispered, her voice trembling. "I didn't ask for this."

The voice was quiet for a moment, but then it spoke again, colder this time. "It does not matter what you want. The bond cannot be undone. You will always be part of the Nexus."

Alara's hands clenched into fists at her sides as the full weight of the voice's words settled over her. The Nexus wasn't just a place—it was alive, sentient, and it had chosen her. There was no escaping it.

But Alara wasn't willing to accept that. Not yet.

"No," she said, her voice firm. "I won't be controlled by you. I'll find a way out of this."

The voice chuckled darkly, a sound that sent a shiver down her spine. "You cannot escape the Nexus, Alara. It is everything. It is time itself. And you are bound to it for eternity."

Alara's heart pounded in her chest, her mind racing for a way out. She couldn't stay here, trapped in this barren wasteland, forever tied to the Nexus's will. She had to find Leo. She had to find a way to break free.

Without another word, Alara turned and began to walk, her steps quickening as she moved further away from the edge of the cliff. The voice didn't follow her, but she could still feel its presence, lingering in the air like a shadow.

The landscape stretched out before her, endless and unforgiving, but Alara didn't stop. She couldn't. Leo was out there somewhere, and she was going to find him—no matter what it took.

As Alara pressed forward, the barren wasteland seemed to stretch on forever, the cracked earth crunching beneath her feet with every step. The wind whipped through her hair, cold and biting, but she didn't slow down. She couldn't afford to.

Hours passed, or at least what felt like hours. In this strange world, time seemed to have no meaning. The sun didn't move in the sky, and the swirling colors above her remained unchanged. But Alara kept moving, driven by the faint hope that she would find Leo.

But as the minutes turned into what felt like days, doubt began to creep into her mind. What if she couldn't find him? What if the Nexus had taken him from her, pulled him into a different reality, a different timeline?

The thought was unbearable.

Alara's legs ached, her body exhausted from the relentless march through the wasteland. But just as she was about to collapse from sheer exhaustion, something caught her eye in the distance.

A figure.

At first, she thought it was another trick of the light, a mirage conjured by her tired mind. But as she blinked and rubbed her eyes, the figure remained, standing tall on the horizon.

Her heart leaped in her chest as she broke into a run, her feet pounding against the cracked earth as she raced toward the figure.

"Leo!" she shouted, her voice hoarse from disuse.

The figure didn't move, didn't respond, but Alara kept running, her breath coming in short, desperate gasps as she drew closer. And then, finally, she reached him.

But it wasn't Leo.

Alara skidded to a stop, her heart plummeting as she realized who it was.

Standing before her, cloaked in dark energy and with eyes that gleamed with malice, was Veridian.

"Did you really think you could escape?" Veridian sneered, his voice cold and mocking. "You belong to the Nexus now, Alara. There's no escaping that."

Alara's blood ran cold as Veridian's words echoed in her mind. This was impossible. They had defeated him. They had won.

But as she stared into his eyes, filled with hatred and triumph, she realized the truth. Veridian had never truly been defeated. The Nexus had kept him alive, kept him tethered to its power, just as it had done to her.

"You don't control me," Alara said, her voice steady despite the fear that gripped her chest.

Veridian's smile widened, his eyes gleaming. "You still don't understand, do you? The Nexus doesn't just control time. It controls everything. And now… it controls you."

Alara took a step back, her mind racing. "No. I won't let you take control."

Veridian laughed, a sound that sent a shiver down her spine. "It's too late, Alara. You've already given yourself to the Nexus. You and Leo—you're nothing more than tools, pawns in its game. And now, you will serve its will."

Alara's heart pounded in her chest as the full weight of Veridian's words sank in. He was right. The Nexus had bound her to its power, tied her to the flow of time in ways she didn't fully understand. But she wasn't going to let it control her. Not now. Not ever.

"I won't let you win," Alara said, her voice filled with determination.

Veridian's smile faded, replaced by a cold, calculating look. "We'll see about that."

And with that, the ground beneath Alara's feet shifted, and the landscape around her dissolved into a swirling vortex of light and darkness.

Alara gasped, her vision blurring as she was pulled into the vortex, her body weightless as the world around her twisted and contorted. She could feel the pull of the Nexus, stronger than ever, tugging at her mind, trying to bend her will to its own.

But Alara resisted. She wasn't going to give in. Not now, not ever.

With a surge of strength, Alara reached out with her mind, searching for the bond that had once tied her to Leo. It was faint, almost imperceptible, but it was still there—a flicker of light in the darkness.

"Leo," she whispered, her voice filled with desperation. "Please… help me."

For a moment, there was nothing but the roar of the vortex, the swirling chaos of the Nexus threatening to consume her. But then, out of the darkness, a voice echoed in her mind—a voice that sent a wave of relief crashing over her.

"Alara."

It was Leo.

"Leo," Alara whispered, her voice cracking as she reached out with everything she had left. The bond between them flickered weakly, like a dying flame, but it was still there. It was enough.

For the first time since being pulled into the desolate wasteland, Alara felt hope.

"Where are you?" Alara's voice was trembling, but her resolve was firm. She wasn't going to lose him. Not now, not after everything they'd been through.

For a moment, there was only silence. Then, faintly, Leo's voice echoed in her mind again. "I'm here, Alara. I'm... trapped, but I'm here."

Her heart skipped a beat. He was alive. Somehow, somewhere, he was alive. But trapped? What did that mean?

"Trapped where?" she asked, her voice wavering.

Leo's presence was faint, as if he were speaking from a great distance, but his words were clear. "I don't know. The Nexus... it pulled me into something. It's like I'm caught between timelines, between realities. I can see glimpses of them, but I can't move. I can't get out."

A shiver ran down Alara's spine as she tried to imagine what Leo was describing. The Nexus was powerful, far more powerful than they had realized, but it wasn't just a machine. It was alive, sentient, capable of bending time and reality to its will. And now, it had Leo trapped in its web, holding him between worlds, between lives.

"I'm going to get you out of there," Alara said, her voice filled with determination. "I won't leave you."

The bond between them flickered again, a brief pulse of warmth that gave Alara strength. "I trust you," Leo's voice came, faint but sure. "But be careful. The Nexus... it's changing."

Alara's breath hitched in her throat. Changing? What did that mean?

She didn't have time to ask, though, because at that moment, the vortex around her intensified. The swirling light and darkness that had surrounded her since Veridian's appearance began to pull at her more violently, dragging her deeper into the chaos.

For a brief, terrifying moment, she felt like she was being torn apart, like her very essence was unraveling. But then, as quickly as it had started, the sensation stopped.

Alara collapsed onto solid ground, gasping for breath. She was back on the cliff, overlooking the barren wasteland. But something was different. The air was thicker, heavier, and the sky above her was no longer a swirling mass of colors. It was dark, filled with storm clouds that crackled with electricity.

And standing before her, bathed in the flickering light of the storm, was Veridian.

His form was sharper now, more defined than it had been before. The dark energy that surrounded him pulsed with a menacing force, and his eyes glowed with a cold, malicious light.

"You're persistent, I'll give you that," Veridian said, his voice dripping with contempt. "But it doesn't matter. The Nexus has already claimed you. You and Leo."

Alara pushed herself to her feet, her body aching from the strain of the vortex. "You won't win," she said, her voice steady despite the fear that gnawed at her insides. "We're stronger than you think."

Veridian's smile widened, and he took a step toward her. "Stronger? You don't even understand the power you're dealing with. The Nexus doesn't care about your strength or your bond. It's beyond you, beyond anything you can comprehend."

Alara's hands clenched into fists at her sides as anger surged through her. "We've already beaten you once. We'll do it again."

Veridian's eyes narrowed, and for the first time, Alara saw a flicker of doubt cross his face. "You may have won a battle," he said, his voice low, "but the war is far from over. The Nexus is infinite. Its power is limitless. And you are nothing more than a pawn in its game."

Alara took a step forward, her gaze locked on Veridian's. "We're not pawns. We're not tools for the Nexus to use. We'll find a way to stop it."

Veridian's laughter echoed through the air, cold and mocking. "Stop it? You can't stop the Nexus, Alara. It's time itself. It's the very fabric of existence. You think you can defy time?"

Alara's heart pounded in her chest, but she refused to back down. "I think we can find another way. A way that doesn't involve becoming its slaves."

Veridian's smile vanished, replaced by a look of pure hatred. "You're a fool if you believe that. The Nexus will consume you, just as it has consumed everyone who came before you."

Alara's breath caught in her throat as his words sank in. Everyone who came before… What did he mean by that?

Veridian seemed to sense her confusion, and his smile returned, darker and more sinister than before. "Ah, I see you didn't know. You're not the first, Alara. The Nexus has claimed many before you. Some were powerful, like you. Others… less so. But they all shared the same fate."

Alara's mind raced as she tried to process what Veridian was saying. If he was telling the truth, then the Nexus had been trapping people for centuries, maybe even millennia, pulling them into its web, binding them to its power.

"What happened to them?" Alara asked, her voice barely more than a whisper.

Veridian's eyes gleamed with malice. "They became part of the Nexus, just as you will. Their identities were erased, their lives absorbed into the flow of time. They are the Nexus now, bound to its will for eternity."

Alara's stomach churned at the thought. Was that what awaited her and Leo? To be absorbed into the Nexus, to lose themselves completely, to become nothing more than memories in the vast, endless stream of time?

"No," she said, her voice shaking with anger. "That's not going to happen to us."

Veridian raised an eyebrow, clearly amused by her defiance. "Oh? And what makes you so sure?"

Alara took a deep breath, her resolve hardening. "Because we're not like them. We're not going to let the Nexus control us."

For a moment, Veridian said nothing, his eyes studying her intently. Then, slowly, he began to laugh, a low, chilling sound that sent a shiver down Alara's spine.

"You truly believe you have a choice, don't you?" Veridian sneered. "You still think you can fight this. How amusing."

Alara's hands clenched into fists, but she forced herself to stay calm. She wasn't going to let Veridian get under her skin. Not this time.

"You don't understand the power of the bond we share," Alara said, her voice steady. "Leo and I—our connection is stronger than anything the Nexus can throw at us. We're not going to let it take us."

Veridian's laughter died away, replaced by a cold, calculating expression. "We'll see about that."

Before Alara could respond, the ground beneath her feet trembled, and the sky above them darkened even further. The air crackled with electricity, and the familiar hum of the Nexus filled her ears once more.

But this time, it was different. The energy of the Nexus wasn't distant or far away. It was close—so close that Alara could feel it in her bones, in her very soul.

And then, without warning, the bond between her and Leo flared to life, brighter and stronger than ever before. It surged through her, filling her with a warmth and strength that she hadn't felt since the moment they had stabilized the Nexus.

"Leo," she whispered, her heart swelling with hope.

She could feel him again. He was alive, and he was fighting just as hard as she was.

The bond pulsed again, and this time, it brought with it a flood of emotions—love, determination, fear, and, most of all, hope. Leo was reaching out to her, calling her name, fighting to reconnect with her.

"Alara, I'm here," his voice echoed in her mind, clear and strong.

Tears filled Alara's eyes as she reached out with her thoughts, strengthening the bond between them. "I'm here too, Leo. I'm not giving up on you."

The bond pulsed again, and for the first time since being pulled into the Veil, Alara felt like they had a chance. They weren't just pawns in the Nexus's game. They were connected, bound by something stronger than time itself.

Veridian watched them with narrowed eyes, his expression unreadable. "You think your bond can save you?" he said, his voice dripping with disdain. "The Nexus is stronger than both of you."

But Alara wasn't listening. She could feel Leo's presence growing stronger with every passing second, the bond between them solidifying into something unbreakable.

"We're stronger together," she said, her voice filled with conviction.

And then, with a surge of determination, Alara reached deep into the bond, pulling on every ounce of strength they shared. The energy of the Nexus roared around them, but Alara didn't falter. She focused on Leo, on the connection they had, and used it to push back against the dark energy that surrounded them.

Veridian's eyes widened in shock as the bond flared to life, brighter than ever before. The dark energy that had once surrounded them began to dissipate, retreating in the face of the power they shared.

"No!" Veridian snarled, his voice filled with rage. "You can't do this!"

But Alara and Leo stood firm, their bond unshakable. Together, they pushed back against the Nexus, against Veridian, against the darkness that had threatened to consume them.

And then, with one final burst of energy, the bond between them exploded outward, engulfing the entire landscape in a brilliant light.

When the light faded, the barren wasteland was gone. The storm clouds had cleared, and the sky above them was a brilliant, clear blue.

Alara gasped, her body trembling with exhaustion as she collapsed into Leo's arms. He held her tightly, his chest heaving with exertion as they both tried to catch their breath.

"You did it," Leo whispered, his voice filled with awe. "You saved us."

Alara smiled weakly, her heart swelling with relief. "We did it," she corrected, her voice barely more than a whisper.

Together, they had fought back the Nexus, defeated Veridian, and emerged victorious. But as they stood there, holding each other in the quiet aftermath, Alara couldn't shake the feeling that their journey wasn't over.

The Nexus was still out there, still watching, still waiting.

And deep down, she knew that the real battle had only just begun.

The Nexus had quieted, its relentless energy finally subsiding into a gentle hum that echoed faintly in the air. Alara and Leo stood together, their bodies exhausted but their spirits triumphant. They had faced Veridian, the dark force that had sought to enslave them to the Nexus, and they had won. For now.

But as Alara leaned into Leo's embrace, her heart still racing from the intensity of the battle, she couldn't shake the gnawing feeling that something wasn't right. Despite their victory, the world around them didn't feel as it should. The air still hummed with the presence of the Nexus, an unsettling reminder that they had only scratched the surface of its true power.

"We did it," Leo whispered, his voice heavy with relief. "But why doesn't it feel like it's over?"

Alara pulled back slightly, looking into his eyes. "Because it's not. The Nexus is still here… watching. Waiting."

Leo frowned, his grip tightening around her as he glanced around the now calm landscape. "You think Veridian was just the beginning?"

Alara nodded, her mind racing with possibilities. The Nexus had bound them to itself, but what if that connection was only part of something much larger—something they hadn't even begun to understand?

"The Nexus isn't just about controlling time," she said softly. "It's more than that. There's something deeper, something we haven't uncovered yet."

Leo's brow furrowed as he considered her words. "Deeper? Like what?"

Alara hesitated, the weight of the Nexus's presence pressing down on her chest. "I don't know," she admitted. "But I can feel it. There's something... hidden, something we're not seeing."

For a long moment, neither of them spoke. The sky above them was clear, and the strange colors that had once swirled through the atmosphere had vanished. But despite the calm, there was an undeniable tension in the air—a sense of unfinished business, of unresolved mysteries lurking just beyond their reach.

"What do we do now?" Leo asked, his voice laced with uncertainty.

Alara bit her lip, her mind turning over the endless possibilities. They had stabilized the Nexus, fought off Veridian, and emerged victorious. But they were still bound to it, tied to its power in ways they couldn't fully comprehend. And if the Nexus wasn't finished with them yet, then what came next?

"I don't know," she said quietly. "But I think... I think we have to keep going. There's more to the Nexus than we realize, and if we don't figure it out, we might never be free."

Leo's expression darkened, his eyes flickering with uncertainty. "You think we can get free?"

Alara's heart ached at the question. She wanted to believe that they could—that one day, they would find a way to sever their connection to the Nexus and return to their normal lives. But deep down, she knew that things would never be the same. The Nexus had changed them, bound them to its power, and it wasn't going to let them go easily.

"I don't know," she whispered. "But we have to try."

They stood there in silence, the weight of their situation pressing down on them like a heavy fog. Alara could feel the pull of the Nexus in the back of her mind, always present, always watching. It was like a shadow that she couldn't escape, no matter how far she ran.

But then, out of the silence, a sound—a faint whisper, so soft that Alara almost missed it.

Her breath caught in her throat as she turned, her eyes scanning the landscape for the source of the sound. It was coming from the Nexus—the crystalline structure that had once pulsed with such overwhelming energy, now quiet and still.

"Do you hear that?" Alara asked, her voice trembling.

Leo nodded, his face pale. "Yeah. What is it?"

Alara took a hesitant step toward the Nexus, her heart pounding in her chest. The whisper grew louder, though she still couldn't make out the words. It was as if the Nexus was trying to tell her something, something important—something that could change everything.

"I think it's trying to show us something," Alara said, her voice barely above a whisper.

Leo frowned, his eyes filled with uncertainty. "Show us what?"

Before Alara could respond, the ground beneath their feet trembled, and the Nexus flared to life once more. The air crackled with energy, and a blinding light erupted from the crystal, engulfing them both.

Alara gasped, her vision blurring as the light consumed her. But even as the world around her dissolved into chaos, she could feel it—the presence of the Nexus, stronger than ever, pulling at her, showing her something she had never seen before.

And then, in a flash of clarity, she understood.

The Nexus wasn't just a tool. It wasn't just a machine that manipulated time.

It was alive.

Alara's eyes snapped open, and the world came rushing back into focus. She was still standing beside Leo, her heart racing, but the Nexus had gone quiet once more. The light was gone, the energy had faded, and everything around them was still.

But Alara knew now. She understood.

"The Nexus is alive," she whispered, her voice trembling with the weight of the realization.

Leo's eyes widened in shock. "What do you mean? Alive... like a person?"

Alara shook her head, her mind still reeling from the revelation. "No. Not a person. But it's not just a machine, either. It's... conscious. It has its own will, its own purpose."

Leo stared at her, his expression filled with disbelief. "But how? How can something like the Nexus be alive?"

Alara didn't have an answer. All she knew was that the Nexus wasn't what they thought it was. It wasn't just a tool for manipulating time. It was something far more powerful, far more dangerous.

And they were still bound to it.

"We need to leave," Leo said, his voice urgent. "We need to get out of here."

Alara nodded, her heart racing. But as they turned to leave, the air around them shimmered, and the whisper returned—louder this time, more insistent.

"You cannot escape..."

The voice sent a chill down Alara's spine. It was the same voice she had heard before, the one that had warned her about the bond. But now, it was stronger, more commanding.

"The Nexus is alive," the voice whispered, echoing through the air. "And you are part of it now."

Alara's breath caught in her throat as the full weight of the voice's words sank in. They weren't just bound to the Nexus—they were part of it. And no matter how hard they tried, they could never truly escape.

Leo's face paled as the realization hit him too. "Alara... what does this mean?"

Alara's heart ached as she looked at him, her eyes filled with sorrow. "It means... we're not done. There's more to this than we ever imagined."

The air around them grew heavier, the presence of the Nexus pressing down on them like a vice. The voice whispered again, louder this time, filling the space around them with its ominous presence.

"You are the key," it said. "You always have been."

Alara's heart raced as she tried to make sense of the voice's words. The key? What did that mean?

And then, just as suddenly as it had begun, the whisper faded, leaving behind a deafening silence.

Alara and Leo stood together, their hands still clasped, their minds reeling from the revelation. The Nexus was alive. And they were the key.

But to what?

Alara didn't know the answer, but one thing was clear—they weren't finished. The Nexus had more secrets to reveal, more mysteries to uncover. And whatever lay ahead, it was far more dangerous than anything they had faced before.

As they stood there in the silence, the weight of the Nexus pressing down on them, Alara couldn't help but wonder: What would they discover next?

The answer would have to wait.

For now.

Chapter - 20
Epilogue: Echoes Of The Unknown

The Nexus was silent.

For the first time since Alara and Leo had encountered its immense power, the overwhelming hum of energy that had always surrounded them was gone. The air was still, the sky an impossible shade of deep blue, and the world around them seemed peaceful—too peaceful.

Alara stood at the edge of the cliff, staring out at the horizon. The barren wasteland that had once stretched before them had shifted into something else, something that felt more like a dream than reality. Soft, golden light bathed the landscape, and a gentle breeze whispered through the air, carrying with it a sense of calm that seemed almost unnatural.

But Alara couldn't shake the unease that had settled deep in her chest. The calm was a facade. She knew that. The Nexus was alive. It was watching, waiting, biding its time.

And it wanted something from them.

"What do you think it means?" Leo asked softly, standing beside her, his voice low.

Alara glanced at him, her brow furrowed. "The Nexus?"

Leo nodded, his gaze fixed on the horizon. "The voice. It said we were the key."

Alara took a deep breath, her mind racing. The voice had spoken those words with such certainty, as if their entire journey had been leading to this moment. But what did it mean? What were they the key to?

"I don't know," she admitted, her voice barely more than a whisper. "But I don't think we've seen the last of it. The Nexus isn't finished with us."

Leo's jaw tightened, and he turned to face her, his eyes filled with concern. "Do you think we'll ever be free of it?"

Alara wanted to say yes, to reassure him that they would find a way to break free from the Nexus's grip, to return to their normal lives. But she couldn't. The bond between them and the Nexus was too strong, too deep. It was a part of them now, whether they liked it or not.

"I don't know," she said quietly. "But I think we're tied to it, for better or worse."

Leo sighed, running a hand through his hair. "I just want to understand. Why us? Why now?"

Alara had asked herself that same question countless times since their journey had begun. Why had the Nexus chosen them? What had set them apart from all the others who had come before?

"I think... we're missing something," she said slowly, her mind piecing together fragments of thoughts that had been swirling in her head since they first encountered the Nexus. "Something important. We've only scratched the surface of what the Nexus is capable of."

Leo frowned, his brow furrowed in confusion. "What do you mean?"

Alara turned to face him fully, her eyes intense. "Think about it. The Nexus can control time. It can manipulate reality. But we haven't even begun to understand how deep its power goes. What if... what if it's more than just controlling time? What if it's controlling us?"

Leo's eyes widened in shock. "You think the Nexus is manipulating us?"

Alara nodded, her mind racing with possibilities. "What if every decision we've made, every choice we thought was our own, was really the Nexus guiding us? Pushing us toward something?"

Leo's face paled as he considered her words. "But why? What could it possibly want from us?"

Alara swallowed hard, her heart pounding in her chest. "That's what we need to figure out."

The world around them shimmered for a brief moment, the soft golden light flickering as if it were nothing more than a projection. Alara's breath caught in her throat as she felt the familiar pull of the Nexus, tugging at the edges of her consciousness. It was faint, almost imperceptible, but it was there.

"I feel it too," Leo whispered, his voice tight with fear.

Alara closed her eyes, focusing on the bond between them and the Nexus. It was still there, still pulsing faintly in the back of her mind, a constant reminder that they were never truly free. But now, there was something else—a presence, lurking just beneath the surface, waiting for the right moment to reveal itself.

"The Nexus is waking up," Alara said, her voice trembling. "It's been dormant, but now... now it's coming back."

Leo's grip tightened on her hand, his eyes wide with fear. "What do we do?"

Alara took a deep breath, her mind racing. They couldn't run. They couldn't hide. The Nexus was part of them now, and there was no escaping its reach.

"We need to confront it," she said, her voice steady despite the fear that gnawed at her insides. "We need to find out what it wants."

Leo hesitated for a moment, his gaze flickering between her and the shimmering horizon. "And if we don't like the answer?"

Alara's heart clenched at the thought. If the Nexus had been manipulating them all along, guiding their every move, then whatever it wanted from them couldn't be good. But they didn't have a choice. They had to face it.

"We'll deal with that when the time comes," she said softly. "But we can't let it control us. Not anymore."

Leo nodded, his jaw set with determination. "Together, then."

"Together."

The walk toward the Nexus felt longer this time, as though the landscape was stretching out before them, making the distance greater with every step. Alara's heart raced in her chest, her mind swirling with questions. What was the Nexus? Why had it chosen them? And what did it mean when it called them the key?

The bond between them and the Nexus pulsed faintly in the back of her mind, a constant reminder of the connection they couldn't escape. But now, it felt different. Stronger. More insistent.

As they approached the heart of the Nexus, the crystalline structure that had once shimmered with an otherworldly light was dark, its surface cold and lifeless. But Alara could feel it, deep within the core of the structure—an energy, a presence, waiting to be awakened.

"It's here," Leo whispered, his voice barely audible.

Alara nodded, her breath catching in her throat as she reached out with her thoughts, touching the edge of the Nexus's consciousness. The moment her mind brushed against it, a wave of energy surged through her, and the ground beneath their feet trembled.

The crystalline structure flared to life, its surface glowing with a brilliant, blinding light. The air around them crackled with electricity, and Alara could feel the Nexus's presence pressing down on her, suffocating in its intensity.

"Alara!" Leo shouted, his voice filled with panic.

But Alara couldn't move. She was frozen in place, her mind locked in a battle with the Nexus's overwhelming power. The bond between them surged, stronger than ever before, and Alara realized with a sudden, horrifying clarity that the Nexus wasn't just alive—it was sentient. And it had been waiting for this moment.

"You are the key," the voice whispered, echoing through her mind. "You have always been the key."

Alara's heart pounded in her chest as the words repeated over and over, the meaning still just out of reach. The key. But the key to what?

As the energy of the Nexus pulsed around her, Alara's vision blurred, and for a brief moment, she saw something—something hidden deep within the Nexus, something ancient and powerful, waiting to be unleashed.

And then, just as quickly as it had begun, the vision vanished, leaving Alara gasping for breath.

"What... what was that?" Leo asked, his voice trembling.

Alara shook her head, her mind still reeling from the intensity of the vision. "I don't know. But whatever it is, it's been waiting for us."

The air around them hummed with energy, and Alara could feel the Nexus watching them, its presence more powerful than ever. It was waiting for something—for them to make the next move.

"What do we do now?" Leo asked, his voice filled with uncertainty.

Alara stared at the crystalline structure before them, her mind racing. The Nexus had chosen them, bound them to its power, and now it was waiting—waiting for them to unlock whatever lay hidden within.

But Alara wasn't sure she wanted to know what that was.

"We keep going," she said softly, her voice steady despite the fear that gnawed at her insides. "We figure out what the Nexus wants, and we decide if we're willing to give it."

Leo's eyes widened in shock. "What if it's something we can't give?"

Alara took a deep breath, her heart pounding in her chest. "Then we find a way to fight it."

As they stood before the glowing heart of the Nexus, the energy around them pulsed with a quiet intensity, the air thick with anticipation. The bond between Alara and Leo flared to life, stronger than ever before, and Alara knew that whatever came next would change everything.

But as they prepared to take the next step, the ground beneath their feet trembled once more, and the voice of the Nexus whispered in the air around them.

"You are the key. You must choose."

Alara's breath caught in her throat as the meaning of the words finally clicked into place. The Nexus wasn't just waiting for them—it was giving them a choice. A choice that would shape the future of everything.

But what that choice was, and what the consequences would be, was still a mystery.

And as the light of the Nexus pulsed brighter and brighter, Alara realized that they were about to discover the truth.

Ending Words From The Author

A Message from the Author: A Journey Just Beginning

Dear Readers,

As we reach the final page of *Beyond Time's Veil*, I want to extend my heartfelt gratitude to each and every one of you for joining me on this incredible adventure. This story has been shaped by mystery, time, and the bonds of love. It has been more than just a tale—it's been a piece of my heart, and I'm deeply honored to share it with you.

Before we move forward, I must take a moment to acknowledge the person who inspired this journey: my grandfather, **Late. Shivaji S. Kakade**. His wisdom, guidance, and belief in me have been the driving force behind this book. Throughout my life, he has been a

beacon of strength and inspiration, and it is because of him that this story found its way onto these pages. I hope this book carries forward the values he instilled in me—curiosity, resilience, and the courage to explore the unknown.

As we've followed Alara and Leo through the mysteries of the Nexus, we've only scratched the surface of what lies ahead. The Nexus has revealed its power and hinted at deeper secrets, but the truth is far more complex than we can imagine. While many questions remain unanswered—what is the true purpose of the Nexus? Why were Alara and Leo chosen?—I promise you, the answers are coming, and they will be beyond anything you could have expected.

The adventure continues in **"Beyond Time's Veil, Part II: The Nexus Unbound."** In this next chapter, Alara and Leo will delve deeper into the heart of the Nexus, uncovering realities that challenge the very fabric of time and existence. Their connection to the Nexus will be tested, and what they discover will push them to the limits of their courage and strength. But with great power comes great danger, and the Nexus is not done with them yet.

What lies ahead is both exhilarating and terrifying. The Nexus has been waiting for them—and now that it's awake, nothing will ever be the same again. In **"Beyond Time's Veil, Part II: The Nexus Unbound,"** we will explore the true depths of the Nexus and the immense power it holds. But Alara and Leo's journey is also one of self-discovery, of unearthing what it means to truly hold the key to the future.

I am beyond excited to share this next part of the journey with you, and I want to thank you for being a part of it from the beginning. Your support and curiosity mean the world to me. As we continue, I hope the story captivates you even more, that it stirs your imagination, and that it connects with you on a deeper level—just as my grandfather's inspiration has connected with me.

So, as we prepare to journey further into the unknown, remember: this is just the beginning. The Nexus has more secrets to reveal, and the next steps will change everything.

Thank you again for your unwavering support, and I can't wait to take you deeper into this adventure in **"Beyond Time's Veil, Part II: The Nexus Unbound."**

With all my heart and in loving memory of my grandfather,

Vaishnav Shailesh Kakade

www.ingramcontent.com/pod-product-compliance
Lightning Source LLC
LaVergne TN
LVHW041911070526
838199LV00051BA/2577